ANYTIME THE BIRDS FALL

DANIELLE STEWART

ANYTIME THE BIRDS FALL

Marta is on the verge of a new life. Hard earned success waits just around the next corner. But only if she's brave enough to keep walking toward it. Winning the Milton Cesar Foundation for the Arts Award will launch her career. With the spotlight turned her way, she'll have to face a messy past and dream of a brighter future.

Carol is burdened with the desire to fix what's broken. To make room for more people in the elite foundation she currently runs. But change is hard and the people around her don't share her vision. Selecting Marta as the award recipient was a bold step. Getting everyone on board seems an insurmountable task.

The two must come to terms with their collective fears. If they plan to change anything, they must face everything. Danger included. With Robert and Terrance by their sides, there is room for hope. For possibility. Maybe even for love.

1

Marta

An award should evoke a celebratory feeling. In the face of all the seemingly endless barriers, Marta had done it. She'd not only written a book and put it out into the world. Somehow, it had been selected for recognition by the Milton Cesar Foundation for the Arts. A prestigious career launching accolade that would certainly alter her life.

There should have been dancing on the table and corks popping off bottles of champagne. Instead there were meticulous plans to be made. Emotional fields full of land mines that had been placed long ago. An ex-husband with a vendetta. A mother with more baggage than a cross country greyhound bus. A town who considered her a failure. People who would line up to spill the tea on her past in a very public way. And an industry who would certainly find her wholly unworthy of such praise. Today, Marta was a small town self-made woman who'd found a way to prop herself up and outrun the trauma of her childhood. If she accepted the award, the spotlight of the world was shone upon her. Surely all they would see were the endless flaws and failures she'd worked so hard to plaster up and paint over.

Saying yes should have been the easy part. Who wouldn't say, elevate my career and change the trajectory of my life. It should have rolled off Marta's tongue. Instead she'd spent every waking second since Carol, the CEO of the foundation, first approached her, wondering if she could really pull this off. Was the book actually good? Would the world let a woman like Marta into their elite club of award winning authors?

There had been so many moments of her life that made her question the possibility. The amount of rebuilding and running she'd done to survive should have disqualified her from hope. From the idea of something finally going her way. And in such a big way. It was like climbing out of a dark abyss to find yourself on a mountain top. Implausible. Impossible.

But Carol persisted and insisted. A powerful woman with a completely different life experience who saw promise in Marta she couldn't possibly see in herself. It all felt too good to be true. Too scary to actually accept. Yet for the first time in Carol, and her assistant Terrance, Marta found people unwilling to give up on her. Promotors instead of detractors. There was a chance Carol could be the mother

Marta never had. Terrance could be the man who kept her safe instead of chronically afraid of the next wicked thing that might befall her.

Terrance had swooped in. Stood tall. Spoke kindly. Kissed her perfectly. Convinced her she was worthy. It was almost enough. It sparked something in her. A glimmer of hope. How great it would be to find out all along she was good enough. Or like everything else, it could crumble in her hands and blow away like the dust of her previous heart-breaks and failures.

Marta – Age 9

The head of the hammer smelled of rust and the wooden handle was split in a few places. Marta gripped it tightly anyway. She was unafraid of splinters. Or maybe just less afraid of them than of her father's reaction to any hesitation around tools. Being a designated assistant for a variety of his jobs wasn't Marta's choice. She was both unwilling and painfully unqualified for almost all of the tasks. Her hands were too small. Her skills undeveloped. It didn't usually end well.

Yet, they kept up this routine every time there was something new to be done. If she was holding a flashlight, it was never pointed where he needed it. Her hands would grow tired and start to shake. Handing over a wrench, it was always the wrong size. Her father somehow imagined this girl, not having attended a trade school by the age of nine, was equipped to help him fix a furnace or hand him shingles at the top of the ladder.

No was not an option. There was an unspoken contract that when told to help, you helped. She didn't bother suggesting her tiny frame was not capable of lifting shingles. Or that her inexperience might make it impossible for her to know where the spark plug should go. She'd heard in church that some people believed all things were possible through Christ. Her father believed all things were possible because *what other choice did they have?*

Calling a repairman cost money they couldn't spare. Buying the right tools was out of the question. You made things work with what you had, and Charlie Leduc had free labor in the form of his children.

Her brothers had smartened up. They listened intently as their father would grumble about something loose or broken or acting up. Then they'd hightail it out of the house and stay gone all day. She imagined right now as she clutched the hammer that her brothers were in the loft of the Wilsons' barn reading comics.

"You going to give it to me?" Charlie barked. Whenever he was working on something, he was unrecognizably cranky. The jovial man who would hoist Marta onto his shoulders and playfully march her around was gone the moment he had to shimmy himself up a ladder or under a car.

At this moment, his large frame was wedged precariously under the family's 1971 green Gremlin. The exterior was more Bondo than metal now, and most days it required extraordinary measures to function. Every car they'd ever had for as long as Marta remembered was like this. Temperamental and unreliable. When she was little, the family only had one car. Her parents would have to juggle everything around to make sure they could both get to and from work. It was the cause of fights sometimes. Though they were never short on things to argue about. Since the divorce, they now needed two cars. They had the same amount of money to spend which meant two even worse cars than the one they used to share.

The day this green car chugged and lurched into the driveway of her father's apartment building, Marta held her breath. Not only to block out the exhaust fumes. She also knew this would be the start of something. More afternoons spent trying desperately to keep this car alive. Like a fraught ER doctor, sweat on his brow and electric paddles in his hands, her dad would have to will this car to keep running. And she'd have to be a part of that.

Charlie wasn't a mechanic. He never had the right tools. The jack lifting the car looked as ill-equipped for its job as Marta did for hers.

"Here," she said, placing the hammer in his extended hand that poked out from under the car. The vehicle practically rested on his belly as he maneuvered to bang the starter a few times with the hammer. It hadn't been working lately. This normally reliable fix had failed them the last few times. Closing her eyes and holding her breath, she was desperate for it to be effective today.

While the banging sound of metal on metal hurt her ears, she didn't cover them. Even though Charlie couldn't see her, she felt compelled to be brave. Weakness in his eyes was dangerous. If she showed she couldn't take the sound he was making, how would she be able to repair her own car someday when the starter began to act up?

Charlie wasn't heartless. He didn't push his children because he enjoyed watching them struggle or hurt. He'd grown up in a certain version of the world. Unforgiving, plagued by bad luck, a new seemingly insurmountable challenge around every corner. Charlie knew his children would be subjected to the same. It was his job to make them sturdy enough to survive as if they were houses he was tasked to build, and a hurricane was always on the horizon. Weak walls and a poor foundation wouldn't do. For a sometimes silly guy with a hearty laugh, he took this job very seriously.

His children had to know which wrench to use and how to ignore the pain in their ears at the sound of a loud bang. Dirty jobs couldn't scare them off. It was never even a consideration that his children might have cars that started every time without fail or enough money to hire an actual mechanic. Because of who they were, he knew for sure their toilets would need to be tinkered with and their sinks would leak. Something too fantastical to imagine. So instead, he'd prepare them.

"Go turn the ignition," he snapped, and she could see him shifting his weight. This position, his back flat on the pavement, was clearly uncomfortable. His face was likely covered now with little speckles of rust. A dirty job, but the car was a necessity.

"Are you going to get out of there?" Marta asked, peeking under to see him better.

"I'm not sliding out of here just to find out this didn't work and then have to get back under. Just put the clutch down, keep a foot on the brake and turn the key."

An urgent desire to protest rolled up in her chest but stopped at the back of her throat. There was a gatekeeper there. A little troll that decided if what she planned to say would make things worse or better. Fear gripped tightly around her neck and squeezed. She knew which was the clutch and which was the brake. Logically, she understood what he was telling her to do, but all she could imagine was the horrific scene that would unfold if she hit the wrong pedal and ran her father over. "Can't you come out of there first?"

"Marta, stop second-guessing yourself. You've driven this car before. Why do you think I let you do that? Joy rides? No, you need to know these things."

Driving the car at her age had been exciting. The way almost everything her father thought up seemed at the time. Lately, her impression of his ideas was changing. "But can't I know these things and not run you over?" There was a little snap to her voice, something between a protest and a plea.

"You're not going to run me over." His voice was muffled by the car lying on top of him. But she knew already what he was about to say. “High stakes mean better results.”

Charlie said that often. Marta sometimes wanted to believe him. The more there was on the line, the harder you’d work. But sometimes it only meant her hands would sweat more and her stomach would knot up. She never felt prepared under pressure. Just squeezed tighter.

“You shouldn’t be under there when I start it up.” This had been happening more lately. Marta had surpassed Charlie in good judgment. When she was little, back when she was eight, and Charlie told her to do something, she obeyed. It was easy to trust that he, as the adult, knew what was safe or right. Now, as each month passed, Marta understood that was not true for every adult. Especially for Charlie.

“Get in the car and start it up.” There was a finality in his voice that she wasn’t equipped to argue with.

A familiar sensation rushed through her and she wished it had a name, or a name she knew. It was prickles all over her scalp. That blinky feeling that came before tears, though she knew better than to cry. A lump, a real one, in her throat. She often wondered where the lump went on the rare occasion when she wasn’t afraid. What was it made of? How did it know to come back and clog her throat?

“If I run you over, I’m just going to keep driving until I hit Florida.” This wasn’t exactly the antidote for fear. Humor was more like putting a Band-Aid on a broken bone. Performative and ineffective, but at least an attempt to make things better. When Marta had no control, she had jokes.

"Just hop out and get my wallet first."

"Why? We both know it's empty." Marta kicked at his leg lightly and then dragged herself, lead feet and shaking hands, to the driver's side of the car. It was at an odd angle since it was jacked up, and she found it hard to pull the heavy door open.

"Today, kid. Stop daydreaming," Charlie said, but his voice was gentler now. "Clutch, brake, turn the key."

Daydreamer was a familiar accusation tossed at Marta. They called her imaginative. Creative. This talent that made her able to write stories for school and play endlessly with her thrift shop dolls was actually a curse, not a blessing. The same mind that allowed her to create a pretend world full of fictional characters also became adept at excessively worrying as a way to protect herself. If she'd already thought about her house burning down, then if it happened some part of her would be prepared for it. If she'd fretted how bad her parents' next public fight might be, maybe she could endure it more when the time came. While that never proved true, the worry never lessened the sting, it didn't deter her from letting it consume her thoughts.

Marta had two jobs. Two exhausting roles in her family. First, she was to observe it all. Sense the tiny tremors of the far-off danger. Did someone's expression just change suddenly? Would her mother's actions that Monday change her father's mood when they arrived at his house for the weekend? Then her second job kicked in. Take all of that knowledge, all she'd seen, heard, and felt, and do something about it. If her mother was tense over something her father had done, Marta would try to smooth things over. Or she'd take it upon herself to somehow cheer her mother up, a sometimes impossible task. If her brothers seemed ready to needle their father about an unfair rule, she'd head that off before they could push him to the brink. She'd be a distraction. A diversion. A punching bag. Anything the moment called for as long as it resulted in some semblance of happiness for them. Or at a minimum, a crisis averted.

Hyperaware of how people were feeling and personally responsible to do something about it, Marta's tiny body never fully relaxed. She seemed to be the only one who wanted the big family blow-out arguments to stop, or even better, never start. All day her mind oscillated between the possible impending doom that might be just around the corner and the management of emotions for everyone in her orbit.

Right now, she needed this car to start. She needed her father to emerge safely from underneath it. He couldn't be late dropping them off to their mother today. It was a trigger. An excuse for her to behave badly and him to treat her explosive anger as an excuse for his own. Her mother would be on the porch, waiting. Seething. Not because she couldn't wait to have her children back but rather that she couldn't wait for a reason to hate this man even more. To be right in the presence of his wrongness.

His late arrival would be an invitation for chaos. This car, this broken heap of metal that always let them down, had no idea the consequences of its failures.

Marta closed her eyes and imagined what she'd have to

do if the car crushed her father. The whole thing. Who she'd have to call. What it might sound like. Would everyone know she killed her father? Would she go to jail? No one Marta knew could rapid-fire worst-case scenarios in their mind as well as she could.

By the time the key was in the ignition, she was already onto the next problem. She imagined the shouting that would come from the porch of her mother's apartment if the car didn't crush her dad, but they were still late. Would her mother make them go back to court again? Would the police come this time and actually arrest one of them? The lump grew a few more sizes as she started the car.

When the engine roared to life, a brief and fleeting rush of relief washed over her. A moment or two later, her father was out from under the car, haggard and dirty as he pulled open the car door. "I told you," he said smugly. "You didn't run me over."

"We need to get going," Marta sighed, looking at his old plastic watch. "Why aren't the boys back here yet?"

"I'm sure they were just waiting to see if the car would start. They're dodging the hard work."

"If we don't leave in fifteen minutes, we won't make it in time." The comfort and peace evaporated like steam out of a kettle turned cold.

"Listen, if we're late, we're late. Your mother is going to have to deal with that."

Marta hopped out of the car and her father began unwinding the little jack that had been holding it up. "I'm going to go look for the boys." Her stomach growled loudly and she put a hand over it as if that might stifle the sound.

"You didn't eat?" Charlie asked, furrowing his brows. It was a ridiculous question. He knew she hadn't eaten. None of them had. The last sixteen dollars in Charlie's wallet yesterday had gone to paying for the drive-in movie and half the candy aisle at the discount store. They'd pulled up early and walked the whole asphalt plot collecting enough change on the ground for sodas. People always seemed to drop their money in the dark and walking around at dusk to pick it up was their specialty. Once the spare change went to the concession stand, the last of Charlie's money was gone until he got paid on Monday. Spent on fun. On sweets and a silly movie she'd fallen asleep halfway through.

This too had started to bother her. More of Charlie's strange choices in action.

"I'm not hungry," Marta lied. "I'm going to go find the boys so we can go." Marta had begun wondering why they spent the little money they had on what they did. Sixteen dollars could have bought a loaf of bread, some lunch meat, peanut butter, milk. They'd have had plenty of food to get from Friday night to Sunday morning. Maybe even some extra to carry Charlie through the first few days of the week. Instead, they blew it on fun and indulgence. It didn't make sense. Before, when she was smaller, she wouldn't have pondered such things. But now it all stirred questions in her. If they had so little, why did they use it so poorly?

"Did you have fun at the drive-in last night?" Charlie asked as he tossed the old jack into the trunk with a thud. "I didn't get to do much of that when I was a kid. Too many brothers and sisters to have much fun."

"It was the best." Marta smiled. It had been fun. Exciting. The sweets were delicious and the popcorn bucket seemed bottomless. But a few groceries in the fridge would have been nice too.

Marta was off in the direction of the barn where she assumed her brothers were hiding out. They were just another barrier to her completing her job. Keeping the peace. It was all on her, and she couldn't afford to take a day off.

2

Carol – Age Twelve

"It's not baby fat, Dallas." Her mother's shrill voice stopped Carol in her tracks. She pressed her body against the closest mahogany framed beam and hid. She was relieved to have heard the tone of her mother's angry voice before she'd entered the dining room. Like a warning shot to stay away.

Her father, sounding equally annoyed, rebutted the argument. "She's a child. A perfectly healthy one. Francine, don't go putting anything else in her head."

"She's twelve years old," Francine huffed. "She's got a sweet in her hand every time I turn around. I've had to buy her two sizes larger for the last six months. She's on a dangerous path, and it's our job to keep her from that."

"Dangerous path?" Dallas scoffed. "She's enjoying pie, not cocaine."

A throaty little scream escaped Francine. "Do not be crude, Dallas. You know as well as I do that all these events we having coming up this summer are for her. She's on the social scene now. She can't be going in to all these ballrooms with a chubby face covered with pie."

"She won't. We'll have her wash the pie off." He chuckled, but Carol knew it was only going to make things worse.

"Dallas, I know you wanted a son. You've spared no opportunity to remind me that I was not able to give you one. I'm sorry my body was so damaged by having Carol that I could not give you the heir you wanted. But the child we have still needs to be raised properly. She can't take over your companies or lord over our estates—"

Carol wanted to interrupt and shout *why not?* But she knew better. She only mouthed it to herself through gritted teeth.

"Don't be dramatic, Francine. I've never coveted a son or said anything of the sort to you. It's you who brings that up all the time. I love Carol. She's perfect just as she is. I don't want to put so much pressure on her to conform to this world we live in. Let her be a child. Lord knows neither one of us had the opportunity. By the time I was her age, I was learning my father's business and nearly choking to death in ties at every formal dinner my mother threw. I felt like a prize horse being paraded around."

"You were," Francine shot back. "As was I. People from families like ours need to be paired up thoughtfully. The reason for all those dinner parties was so we could meet. Which we did. And our compatibility on so many fronts is what makes our lives flourish today. Look at all we have. We've surpassed the wealth and prosperity of either of our families. That was the goal, and we accomplished it. We have our parents to thank for it. We owe Carol the same. She needs to fit into the proper clothes and act civilized at these events. It's the only way she will find the appropriate person to spend her life with."

"She's twelve," Dallas said again. "Do we really need to start all of this now? I certainly don't want her dating."

"Of course not," Francine said, and Carol could picture her clutching her pearls. "This has nothing to do with such things. It's about being seen. Remembered. Thought of when the time comes. Don't you want Carol to be happy?"

"Of course I do."

"Well, you're mixing up the short-term happiness of stuffing her face with cake and acting like a heathen for the long-term happiness of having a life of prosperity and comfort."

"I don't see why they are mutually exclusive."

Carol felt the pinch on her ear before she heard the clonking steps of Nanny Rita. "I told you to march in there or I'd take you in myself. I guess we have to do it the hard way."

"Not right now," Carol pleaded but it was too late. She was already stumbling into the dining room and catching herself on the nearest velvet-clad chair.

"What in the world?" Francine yelped, jumping to her

feet as though the calamity was painful. "Nanny Rita, what is going on here?"

"She was at it again," Rita explained, gesturing wildly at Carol. "Down at the pond, caked in mud, playing with frogs."

"Oh no," Francine said sharply. "That is your angora sweater. It's imported. Hundreds of dollars wasted."

"As if we don't have more," Dallas said as he winked at Carol. "You should not wear your nice things to play in the pond."

"I don't have any other clothes," Carol said in a pitiful Oliver Twist sort of way. "I tried not to get dirty, but I slipped."

"You should not be down by the pond," Nanny Rita exclaimed.

"That's right," Francine piled on. "How many times do you need to be told? You are not some street child foraging for food. Stay away from that muck and dirt. You're likely to catch something in that water."

"It sounds like she caught frogs," Dallas said through a wild smile.

"And probably a disease," Francine rebutted. "I am finished with this. Your father and I were just talking, and I have reached my limit. I've begged you to please stop acting so foolishly and take what I'm saying seriously. But that hasn't worked. So instead of me telling you what you need to do, I will tell you why you need to do it. Perhaps you're finally old enough to understand." Francine gestured at the floor. "Sit there. I don't want mud on the new chairs."

Carol shuffled to the spot and tried to cover as much of the mud with her hands as possible. She hugged her arms around herself as she finally took a seat, cross-legged and waiting for the yelling to continue. To her surprise, it didn't.

"You are not a child anymore," Francine began. She shot Dallas a threatening look and he didn't interject. "It's time you learn exactly why so much is expected from you."

Francine dismissed Rita with the wave of her hand. A dainty little flick of the wrist that sent Rita stepping backward until she reached the door and turned. She closed it quietly and was gone.

With her beautiful dress whooshing mystically, Francine spun and took a seat on the small formal sofa across from Carol. She lifted the material of her dress slightly so she could cross her legs and then patted it down into place. "There is an order to things, Carol. All things. You know about animals in the wild, right? You seem to be drawn to nature." She punctuated this statement with a set jaw and turned-up nose.

"Yes, ma'am."

"Then you understand there is a food chain. A balance. A hierarchy. If those things become out of balance, what happens?"

"Well, if there aren't enough predators to eat the prey then one species might grow too rapidly and take over. They could eat too much of one kind of vegetation and then run out of food sources. They could deplete entire other species and make them extinct."

Dallas beamed. "My smart girl."

"Yes," Francine cut in. "So you agree there is an important balance to things that must be maintained."

Though it felt like a trap, Carol nodded her agreement.

"We are part of that balance as well." Francine's face was soft and her voice gentle, though it was more acting than genuine. "I didn't decide what family I was born into, just like a lion doesn't pick what animal he will be. Your father had no control over the fact that he was born into the Burgess family. Here we all are. We're very lucky, wouldn't you say? Of all the things we could have been from algae to stink bugs, we're here, lions. Top of the food chain."

Dallas snickered. "I've always wanted to be a sloth, really. Seems like they have quite the life."

"Stop that," Francine demanded, though for as much power as she liked to think she had, Dallas was still in charge of plenty.

"Oh Francine, I'm only teasing you. Go on." He waved, giving her permission to continue.

"We have a responsibility to the rest of the world. Though we didn't choose this life, we must rise up to it. Meet the expectations thrust upon us. When I was your age, I admit, there were a few galas I would have preferred not to attend, a few boys I wish I hadn't had to dance with, but that is the role we must play. We come from a long line of powerful people. Your family has been full of politicians, religious leaders, business pioneers, doctors, and scientists. Doesn't that sound amazing?"

Carol nodded feverishly. Finally, they agreed on something. Carol would love to be any of those things.

"Your father employs hundreds of people. He holds the power to make or break someone's career in the publishing industry. He is a very powerful man."

Carol wanted to chime in. She wanted to say exactly how much she wished for the same for herself someday. If her mother was making the point that in order for Carol to be that successful, she had to straighten up, then maybe it was time. Maybe there was something worth keeping away from the pond for.

"And do you know what I do?" Francine tipped her chin up a little higher. "Do you know what all the women in our family have done for generations?"

"No," Carol whispered. She'd learned everything she could about her father's business dealings but truly she had no idea that her mother did anything at all.

"I make sure your father is someone people want to work with. I hold our family to a high standard, protect our reputation. I navigate every social setting necessary to connect your father with prospective clients and his next big opportunity. This house, and everyone who works in it, answers to me. I ensure that the life we have is sustainable, not just for you but for generations to come. You will be expected to do the same. And while that may sound simple, it is not. You'll need to learn just how to do it. So that whatever family you create someday can function just as ours does. Civility and prudence are not guaranteed. We are the shepherds of these standards. We, the top of the food chain, must keep the balance. It is a great responsibility, and while you may not want it now, it's yours."

Carol dropped her eyes down to the floor. Her father would call this a bait and switch. All the talk of scientists and business leaders was not for her. She could only live on the periphery of such things. Her life, like her mother's, would be one of support and social commitments. In her mind, there would be no substance. No challenge. No joy.

Her father spoke again. "We also have a responsibility to our community. It's why your mother takes you monthly to the shelter."

"Oh, good point." Francine snapped her fingers and grinned. "Yes. Think about the shelter. What do we do there?"

"We bring food and clothes."

"But why?" Francine asked, drawing the words out slowly.

"Because people need food and clothes?" Carol asked hesitantly.

"No," Francine snapped. "People can gather that kind of thing from all sorts of places. Charities and such. There is no shortage of bleeding hearts in the world. We go as an example. When we walk in to that shelter, people look our way, right?"

Carol often felt as though all eyes were on them when they entered the shelter, but she wasn't sure why.

"That's why we go." Francine brushed her hair off her shoulder regally.

Dallas twisted his face up. "So people look at you?"

"No," she sighed dramatically. "Not to be looked at, to be looked up to. The way we are, the life we live, we're setting a standard. Something they can strive toward. Our very presence creates hope. You must take that seriously, Carol. Be the light someone can look toward. Walking in covered in mud, all disheveled like you are—it diminishes the image we've worked so hard to build. You're doing a great disservice to yourself, to the people who might look up to you, and to all of the family members who have worked to bring us to the place we are today. You're carrying a torch, Carol. Don't be the first in our family to let it extinguish."

The visual was enough to jangle loose something in Carol. She wasn't sure if what her mother was saying was right or not. Judging by her father's face, there was some gray and unexplored areas of the conversation. But the idea that she would be the first in a long line of people to screw it up was a seed that planted itself deep inside her brain. Maybe it was more like a parasite.

"Do you understand?" Francine asked, the stern look returning to her face. "No more fighting your destiny. No more ruckus. You're a proper lady; please, let me help you be the best one you can."

"Yes, mother," Carol replied obediently. There had been demands to behave before this. Talk of dirty shoes and messy hair. But this was altogether different. Without knowing everything about the world, Carol had to believe what her mother was saying was true. And if so, she had a calling. One she had to answer.

"Go wash up." Francine snapped her fingers and Nanny Rita reappeared like magic conjured up from thin air. "Make sure these clothes go right in the trash. Tomorrow we have dinner at the Linbenders. You must be well-rested. No puffy eyes."

Nanny Rita's hand was on her shoulder as she ushered Carol out the door and up the stairs to her bedroom. The touch was far gentler now.

"Nanny Rita," Carol asked, the words apparently oozing with the threat of questions.

"Don't ask me," Rita said quietly. "Just listen to your mother."

"Is she right?" Carol whispered as they stepped into her bedroom and closed the door. Nanny Rita peeled the muddy sweater carefully off Carol and didn't answer. "Is my mother, right?" she pressed.

"You're going to grow up to be a proper lady like your mother. You'll run a household like she does. She is right that it is your destiny. You won't learn how to do that from the muddy puddles in the backyard. You should listen to her."

"But," Carol knew Nanny Rita heard the whole conversation. She must have. How else would she know to step back in the room at just the right moment?

"The rest doesn't matter," Nanny Rita snapped back. "The why doesn't matter. All the other people, like me, and how we fit into it is not important. Just do what she says so you can have a good life. Don't waste the opportunity you have."

Carol pressed her lips tightly closed as Nanny Rita reached for the brush. She didn't want to upset the woman who was about to be handling the knots in her hair. That was asking for trouble. "Okay, Nanny Rita. I'll do better. I'll do what my mother wants."

"Good girl." The brushing was tender as Rita hummed a familiar lullaby. "You're the smartest child I've ever met. Do everything your mother tells you, but watch everything your father shows you. That will make you unstoppable, whatever path you choose."

The thought ran deep through Carol. A profound observation she clung to as her head swam with all these new thoughts.

For someone being so kind, Carol wondered why Nanny Rita had made her go into the dining room in the first place. Then she realized. The sweater was ruined. Someone would need to answer for that. Nanny Rita couldn't afford to take the blame or try to cover up what had happened.

When the knots were finally out of her hair, Carol drew in a deep breath. Her mind was filled with a million questions, though none would form with enough clarity to actually ask aloud.

Nanny Rita placed the brush back down on the dresser and folded her hands neatly, hanging them in front of her. "You can be more, Carol."

She didn't say more than your mother. Or more than all the other women in your family who came before you. But the words were enough to make Carol's heart soar. When she was scrubbed clean and sliding between her silk sheets, she didn't wallow in thoughts of the impending doom tomorrow's dinner party would bring. She'd wear the dress.

Sit for however long it took to get her hair set properly. Every *please* and *thank you* would be loud enough for all to hear. She'd smile at the boys and curtsy to the mothers. If she was meant to be something more, it would have to start tomorrow. And she was finally ready.

3

Marta

Jet lag. Time change. She was blaming this feeling on anything she could besides the obvious triggers. Flying home alone from California left her feeling empty in a way she hardly dreamed possible. The West Coast held palm trees and promise. Opportunity abounded there. Distance. Safety. Terrance. New Hampshire was void of all of those things.

Under the threat of torture, Marta would not admit out loud that leaving Terrance had been a challenge. It was a vulnerability she would not allow. If you're standing in the middle of a tornado, you don't start juggling knives. You don't invite more commotion. That's all Terrance could be. No matter how much she enjoyed the kiss they shared,

Marta understood indulging in anything with Terrance would make an already impossible situation even worse. Knowing that and being able to stop thinking about his dark eyes and his smooth brown skin were two very different things.

The contract in her bag seemed to weigh it down. This was the document that would cement the entire deal. Marta would be agreeing to the terms associated with the award, the documentary video and the ceremony. She'd read it, but the legal jargon was way over her head. She assured Terrance and Carol she'd be signing and returning it in the next couple days. There were just a few things she needed to do first.

As she arrived at her mother's apartment, it was time to face one of those tasks. The wooden door was stained with fingerprints and the knob wobbled in her hand as she knocked and turned it at the same time.

"Mom, it's Marta," she called as she stepped inside. The smell, distinct and familiar, took Marta back to her childhood. This wasn't the place where she'd grown up. There was no one single place Marta called home. Moving was common for them, though Marta didn't always know why. Maybe it was eviction or cheaper rent somewhere else. Sometimes it was moving in with her mother's boyfriend, and moving out shortly after. One time it was definitely a feud with someone in the upstairs apartment.

While this place wasn't where she'd lived, the smell was always the same. It was a mix of the dogs, cigarettes, and a mysterious damp stench like laundry left too long in the washing machine. The house was in disarray but not the worst she'd seen it. Dogs, mangy and tiny nipping beasts, yelped from the other side of a baby gate. The pets never made sense to Marta. Wendy didn't love anything or anyone, so why invite more mouths to feed into her home? The most attention the dogs would get was a sharp yell to shut up and a discounted and dented can of expired dog food every day.

Today they were especially wild, but there was no sign of them having gone to the bathroom on the floor. This could sometimes be a leading indicator of her mother's mental state, but not always. Sometimes Wendy's mania resulted in frenzied cleaning. Sometimes the depression zapped the basic motivation to wash a single dish.

"Back here," her mother called. As usual, the house was dark though it was midday. Curtains were pulled closed and only the glow of her mother's television in the back room stood out.

"Hey, Mom," Marta said, flopping onto the couch. Her mother was lounging in her recliner. Smoke had seeped into the mossy green colored fabric and dulled it. It stained the wallpaper. Permeated every pillow and blanket in the house. It was the perfect metaphor for how invasive something toxic could be.

"The author," her mother sang back condescendingly. There was no pride in the words. "You grace me with a visit?"

Marta would not take the bait. That's not what this trip was about. She hated coming back to her hometown, seeing it again for what it really was. The lens of childhood that had made it somehow cozy and welcoming had shattered. Homelessness, drug use, and graffiti were all rampant. Impossible to overlook. The other problem with being back home was the frequency with which you were bound to run into someone you know. A cousin at every supermarket. A high school acquaintance pumping gas in front of you. It was suffocating.

"How've you been?" Marta asked, readying herself for the long-winded answer that usually included the list of people who'd wronged Wendy. There was always someone in the world whose sole purpose was to ruin Wendy Leduc's life.

"Surviving," Wendy replied, a halo of smoke enveloping her. "I'll be better when your cousin Mitch deals with these parking tickets. Two hundred seventeen dollars. Can you believe that? This city has gone to hell. The crooks up at town hall bankrupted the place and now they have the cops out here preying on the citizens by writing parking tickets. Mitch says he can get rid of them for me."

"Isn't Mitch a mailman?" Marta asked, reluctantly peeking her head down the rabbit hole that was her mother's logic. There was normally a fragment of truth or reality but nothing more than that.

"He knows people," Wendy snipped. "And he knows I don't deserve the tickets. I didn't park where they said I did. It's all a scam."

That was one of her mother's favorites. Scam. The catch-all for things she didn't like. The supermarket didn't honor her expired coupon. Scam. Her disability check was late by a day. Scam. Anything that caused her mild annoyance, whether she deserved it or not, fell into that category.

"I'm sure it'll work out." Marta found platitudes and empty comforting phrases seemed to work the best to keep the peace. Noncommittal but non-confrontational was the balance she tried to keep.

"Your brother got that girl pregnant." Between nearly every word she took a long drag on her cigarette. It made the sharpness of her statement seem even nastier.

"His wife, Mom. She's his wife. Your daughter-in-law. That will be your grandchild." Marta plastered on a smile. A melancholy filled her at the idea of a new generation in their family. More people to carry on the dysfunction even longer.

"I hate her." The deep wrinkles around Wendy's lips became more prominent as she threw a sour face. Being on a list of people her mother hated was not a difficult accomplishment. Hardly exclusive. "I told him not to marry her. She's going to ruin his life with that baby. She's got her claws in him now for the next eighteen years at least."

"What's wrong with Samantha? She seems sweet." Marta knew better than to ask such questions. There would be no suitable answer. Nothing rooted in authenticity. The truth was whomever her mother approved of always came down to one singular thing. It didn't matter your ethnicity, religion, gender, sexual orientation, or any of your beliefs and values. Those things did not come under consideration for Wendy. She gave everyone only one litmus test.

If you were nice to Wendy, doted on her, tossed unwarranted compliments at her, then you were good. You were bright. Worthy of love and admiration. She would smile when you walked into a room and speak highly of you when you were gone.

The adverse was true as well. If you had any criticism of Wendy, you were instantly worthless. Selfish. Unintelligent. All of her opinions of people were formed based on what they did to or for her. There was no loyalty, forgiveness, or genuine assessment of someone's true character.

"She's a snot. Thinks she's better than everyone because she's going to nursing school. Like that makes her some kind of big shot. Last time she was here, she didn't even get up to clear the table when we were done eating. I didn't hear a peep from her about the sauce I made."

"A grandchild," Marta said, her eyes wide. "Your son is going to be a dad. That's a big deal."

"It'll be half her." Stubbing her cigarette out in the glass ashtray on the nearby table, she scoffed. "Why are you here anyway?" Marta had done the unthinkable. She challenged Wendy's delusion with facts. That immediately put her mother off and changed this exchange to an adversarial one.

It had seemed to just strike her mother that someone who hadn't made any effort to visit in months was suddenly at her doorstep.

"I want to talk to you."

"Oh, here we go." With a dramatic sigh punctuated by a smoker's cough, her mother shot up to her feet. "What happened now?"

"What's that supposed to mean?" Marta had been incredibly low maintenance over the years. Unlike her brother, she'd never needed bail money. Never asked for anything, even when her abusive husband was waving a gun around the house. But apparently to Wendy, this visit must be some kind of bad news or drama.

"I'm just assuming you're giving up on something else." Wendy waved her hands around animatedly.

"Giving up?" Marta snapped. She could tolerate a lot of nonsense, but how she was defined was still a sensitive subject.

"Keith." Her mother propped a hand on her hip. "I see him quite often. He's practically running the trucking company now. He bought a house over by the football field. I know he traded his truck in for a new one."

"Are you suggesting me getting divorced was some kind of *giving up?* That's rich coming from you."

"Oh, so it's my fault you let a perfectly good guy go because you thought you were too good for this town?" Her barely-there eyebrow rose up and her eyes narrowed.

Here was the problem. Even if Wendy knew the details of Keith's abuse, she would still be taking this stance. She'd have whitewashed and revised history to suit this conversation. That's why Marta hadn't told her the details. It would have changed nothing. Wendy would still take Keith's side and that would hurt far more than carrying the secret herself. But that was the point of this trip. She'd soon be robbed of the right to secrets. Her life, all of it, would be public soon.

"I didn't leave because I thought I was too good for this town. But I came here to talk to you about my book. Something happened."

"Aren't you going to write more? I mean just one?"

"I will write more." Marta bit at the side of her cheek to keep from screaming.

"I gave copies to all the girls at bingo," Wendy beamed. This was the loophole. The part that took Marta the most time to make sense of. Her mother handed out copies of the book to so many people. Doesn't that imply pride? Unfortunately, not. It was exclusively about being the mother of an author, not having a daughter she was proud of. They were two very different feelings.

"The book is doing very well. It has won some local awards over the last few months." Marta snapped her mouth shut suddenly when her mother moved wordlessly to the kitchen. A glass banged hard against the counter and then smashed to the ground.

"Oh hell," Wendy cried. "Damn glasses."

Marta rolled her eyes. There was always something. When the attention moved off her mother, when good news was spoken out loud, she always found a way to interrupt it. Divert it. "Are you okay?" Marta asked, her voice flat. She already knew this was some staged commotion.

"Get the broom. I don't want to cut myself," Wendy demanded, sounding put off.

Obediently, Marta moved to the small utility closet and snatched up the broom and dustpan. She decided it would be better to just come out with the news fully before her mother broke any more dishes or set a dumpster on fire just to avoid having to congratulate Marta. “I won a very big national award. It’s the Cesar Milton Award.”

“Hmm,” Wendy breathed out. Leaning casually against the fridge, she looked down her nose at Marta. This position shift was no accident. Her mother watched her pluck the largest pieces of glass from the floor and then sweep them into the dustpan. Down on her knees, Marta was reminded she was not better than Wendy.

“You’ve heard of it, right?” Marta did the work but kept pushing her mother.

Wendy turned her lips down and shook her head. “No.”

“We’ve watched the award show together,” Marta said, trying to keep her cool. “Remember that actor Mitch Lincoln hosted that year.”

“That wasn’t with me. Probably your father. I haven’t watched it.”

“It was you. You’ve seen it. My book won that award. It’s a big deal. A life-changing event. I’ll be able to write for a career. Everything will change for me.”

“That’s what you’ve always wanted.” Wendy’s words were layered with accusation.

“That’s what most people want. Success. Happiness. And it’s happening for me. I wanted you to know.”

“Marta,” Wendy said, dramatically rolling her eyes. “Of course, you want me to know. It’s the big middle finger you’ve wanted to hold up in my face forever. Well done.” She clapped sarcastically.

“I did this for me, not to hurt you. And you should be

happy for me. Don't you think that would be a better reaction?" Again logic and boundaries were never a good recipe when trying to actually get something done with her mother. But she couldn't help herself.

"Oh, sorry, Princess Marta. I'm not reacting the way you want me to. We're all going to have to change to do what you like now, right?"

"No," Marta sighed in defeat. "I didn't come here for your approval." She reminded herself of that. "I came because it has an impact on you. In the next year, people are going to want to interview you. They are going to want to know about our family. Where we are from. What it was like when we were kids."

Wendy snorted. "Well, which version do you plan to tell them? I'm the villain, right? Your dad was perfect and fun and I was the monster who ruined all the enjoyment all the time."

"We can decide together what we tell them." Marta was determined not to get derailed. She'd gone over this conversation so many times on the flight home from San Diego. "I want to respect your privacy. I don't want it to be a circus for you."

"Just once it would be nice for you to take my side instead of your father's." Wendy scowled as she pointed to a piece of glass Marta had missed.

"Dad is dead, Mom. You won. There are no sides anymore. You're not in the midst of a divorce. It's over."

"Do you really think people around here aren't going to talk? Maybe you can get me and your brother to tell whatever story you want to invent, but people in this town don't forget. They'll be clamoring to be the first in line to tell what happened to your father. What you did."

"Why do you care?" Marta was desperate for the answer. Wendy hated the man. She'd said cruel things in the wake of his death. Ruined the funeral.

"Do those award people know? Do they really know any of it?" The smug expression on her face was nauseating.

"Trust me, I tried to get them to pick someone else," Marta admitted. "You really think I want them looking behind the curtain and seeing all our garbage? Someone is going to ask about Jonah." That was a wretched thing to say. Marta's brother was killed in a car accident when he drove off alone to get away from his parents fighting. He was just a boy and it had been worse than gasoline on an already raging fire in their family.

"No one better ask me about Jonah unless they want to hear how your father and his temper caused that accident. He left the keys in the car. He taught you kids how to drive it, even though you were just children. All that blood is on his hands."

As a family, they'd never talked in detail about that day. There were accusations of fault during some of the biggest blowouts but they'd never actually talked about what happened. She could tell her mother was dying to hand out some more blame. "Your father never cried. Did you know that? He came here, caused a fight, and let his kid crash a car and then never shed a tear."

"He cried, Mom. I saw him."

"Oh, of course you did. There has never been a single time where you weren't on his side. I say the sky is blue, he says it's purple, and you're there backing him up."

"He's dead." Marta rubbed at her temple. "This is not how I wanted this to go. I was coming here so we could maybe get on the same page about what this award might mean to our family and how we can handle the changes coming our way. I did not always defend Dad. I did not always take his side. There never should have been sides drawn in the first place."

"He was an evil man," she hissed. "You don't know how he really was. What he would do to me. And he had everyone fooled. The whole town loved him."

This was the conversation that created the deepest sour pit in her stomach. The one she couldn't handle. "I don't want to go down this road. Please, Mom. I don't want to rehash all the stuff about Dad. I'm sorry you two had such a tough time. It was tough on all of us."

"But he was perfect. The man had the whole town turn against you. You still stick up for him. They think his blood is on your hands and you don't care."

"I care."

"How in the world do you think this is going to work, girlie? These people, the ones from this fancy award place. They roll into Dreven and this whole thing falls apart. Laurel at the laundry mat, she'll tell them you are the reason your father died. That you don't deserve any award. How many of your father's siblings would say the same thing? Half of them? When people get wind of just how juicy your story is, it'll be moths to a flame. Enough moths to carry you away and drop you off the nearest cliff."

For the first time since Marta walked in the door, she and her mother were agreeing on something. "I know that. I'm here trying to make this work. Trying to make all our lives better. Can't we just for once be normal enough to get by? I'm so tired of it. Don't you want better?"

"You're tired?" Wendy asked, refusing to be outdone. "You think you had this terrible childhood. You don't know what I went through in those years. That was my son who died. That was my life your father ruined. And yet you all loved him so much."

"It's not a competition. It wasn't then and it's not now. Why can't we put that in the past and try to move forward? There's actually a path for us now. We just can't blow it."

"You want to play pretend?" Wendy had a dangerously coy smile. "Act like we are the perfect little family?"

"I don't see why we can't be, why does it have to be an act? Glenn and I are grown now. Dad's dead. It doesn't have to be this hard."

"When you kids wake up and realize how bad things were for me, maybe then we can start. I made so many sacrifices for you. You chased off every man who came into my life. I have nothing now. I gave it all to my children and they can hardly be bothered to come see me."

Marta was often unsettled by the idea of perspectives. Warped realities. It made her wonder sometimes if she was wrong. If the way her mother remembered it was more rooted in facts than she realized. "I've got to go," Marta announced, tucking the dustpan and broom back in their place. "Nothing is happening with this yet. Maybe we can get together again soon and talk more."

"I'd like to hear you say it," Wendy demanded, her arms folded across her chest. "For once I'd like to hear you say your father was the problem. I'd like you to realize how bad he treated me."

Marta's relationship with her mother had been tumultuous but predictably so. Also, from a clinical standpoint it wasn't hard to nail down why Wendy was the way she was. Past behavior was a pretty solid predictor of what she might do or say next. It helped Marta be more confident about putting space and boundaries between them.

Wendy was a narcissist who changed her opinions on people as quickly as the wind changes direction. All bad news or trashy gossip was delivered with a devilish grin. Self-serving and the chronic victim, it was impossible to connect with her in any genuine way. Marta had come to terms with the fact that her mother did not have the tools she needed to love someone other than herself. For some reason, as awful as that sounded, Marta could process that.

Her father was a different story entirely. A confusing paradox. Though in retrospect she now understood he had bouts of depression and probably some undiagnosed anxiety, he hadn't fit in any one particular box. Charlie had been a cheerleader. He'd wanted to see other people succeed. No matter how broke he'd been there had been a compulsion to help someone in need. Jovial and quick-witted, he'd made friends easily. When he'd entered a room full of local folks, they'd shouted out his name and raised up their glasses.

What those people didn't see was the dysfunction. Some hard-to-name quirks that had grown into something more troubling over time. What Charlie did better than Wendy was masking it all. He loved outwardly. Exclusively. One hundred percent of what he had was always to be given to others. For most of her life, Marta believed that was what brought him great joy. And perhaps that was somewhat true. Now, after years of reckoning with the mysteries of her father, she could see that the primary reason he left nothing for himself was because he felt as though he was not worthy of it.

When they were nearly penniless themselves, he still donated money to a child in a far-off country in need. He'd repair someone's house when his body was broken and in need of rest. Without an ounce of hesitation, he would sit and listen to the worries and burdens of a neighbor even though he was being crushed by his own.

Charlie asked for nothing. Or more accurately, he insisted on it. He didn't like attention of any kind. No cake on his birthday. Couldn't take him out to a decent dinner. Even when he did have some money to spare from working overtime on a holiday, he wouldn't buy himself clothes or other necessities. He dressed like a pauper. The furniture in his house was always something he'd found discarded and waiting for trash pickup.

The older Marta got, the more embarrassed by these things she became. Nothing was worse than your father rolling up to school in a car that was backfiring and smoking. He'd hang his arm out the window, his paint-covered, holey T-shirt on full display.

Now her mother was asking something of her that Marta could not give. There was too much left to find out about her father. Too many unanswered questions. There was a chance that the depths of his idiosyncratic behavior were worse than she knew. Maybe he had, without Marta seeing, put Wendy through hell. He was imperfect. Confusingly stubborn and seeming in many ways to be self-loathing and chronically deeming himself unworthy. Couldn't that be enough to tax a marriage? Ruin Wendy's life?

"You can't say it," Wendy snarled. "You can't acknowledge your father, the martyr, was imperfect."

"Why is that more important to you than whether or not I'm over the trauma of him dying? Over my part in it. I lost my father. Everyone blames me. Do you think that's been easy?"

"Life's not easy," Wendy replied, offering it more as a slight than advice. "Mine sure hasn't been. He was insane. You don't want to see that. Head in the sand."

"I know he wasn't perfect." Marta conceded. "I saw it. He'd get hung up on the strangest things. He was immovable when it came to those beliefs. We took risks as kids we never should have and usually at his urging. But this opportunity is bigger than the past. Or I hope it is."

Wendy slapped the bottom of her cigarette box on the palm of her hand a few times. "The past, a past like ours . . .

it is too big. It's quicksand. You're trying to build your future on quicksand."

The visual was painfully real. "I know." Marta quieted all the other things she wished to say. The accusations. The clinical diagnosis she'd like to assign to her mother. It didn't matter now. All that was left was the truth. The quicksand she was trying to build on.

4

Terrance

"On a scale of one to ten," Carol asked, her brows crushed together with worry, "One being *she's already crumpled up the contract* and ten being *it's signed and being scanned over now*, give me your best guess."

Terrance smirked. "I know you've got so much on the line here so I'm going to refrain from making jokes about how funny it is to see you this freaked out."

"Please do refrain," Carol sighed.

"I dropped Marta off at the airport and she was very excited about the award. We talked through a few scenarios. She was going to talk to her mother this morning."

"So you're not worried she's going back home, hitting the big brick wall of reality, and ripping up the contract?"

Terrance was absolutely worried that might happen. But his job was not to sink with the ship. His was to bail water and keep them afloat. "I'm going to talk to her this afternoon. I'll offer to fly out and help her with some of the other things she's worried about. I know her ex is a big problem. I'd like to be there to help if that becomes unmanageable for her."

"No violence," Carol insisted. "You're far too gorgeous to engage in a fistfight. I can't have you damaging that perfect jawline."

"First, I don't plan to start a fight, but I'm not walking away from one either if it comes my way. My jaw will be fully intact."

Carol nodded and hummed. "How did things go with you two? You seemed to really hit it off."

"That's what you wanted, right?" Terrance checked his watch and tried to play it cool. "Marta is great. I want this to work out for both of you. I'll do whatever I can to make that happen."

"We need the contract," Carol said somberly. "It's a nonstarter without that. I've received two emails from board members asking if I've secured it yet."

"You've received more than email," Terrance reminded her. "I'm still pretty pissed off that Eli sent you a dead rat to the office. I don't like the idea of letting that go unanswered."

"How does one answer a dead rat in the mail? Do we send threats through rabid carrier pigeons?"

"I'm not ruling anything out." Terrance lowered his

voice. "You're Eli's worst nightmare. You're more competent than he is and no matter how much he digs into your past there isn't anything to exploit. You know that blackmail is his go-to. That worries me. What will he do when none of his normal tricks work?"

"I didn't get this far in my career by cowering to men like Eli. You know how you handle a bully?"

"I do. You sucker punch him when he turns to make a joke about you to his buddies. Then when he's down, you whisper some really over-the-top threat."

"That's very specific."

"I may have dealt with a few in my day. Let me deal with Eli. Keep yourself out of it. Some plausible deniability is always a good thing. I'll keep you out of it."

"You seem to have quite a few dragons to slay all of a sudden. You want to take on my work rivals. Marta's past. Her ex-husband."

"Just doing my part. There are too many men like that out in the world. Small, fragile idiots who think threats and intimidation are the best tools in their toolbox for getting things done."

"Are those not the tools you're going to use?" Carol grinned. "Or were you planning to sit them down and have an adult conversation about boundaries and consent?"

"Plausible deniability." Terrance put his palms down on her desk and leaned in. "You might think Eli is just some blustering old-timer with a few tricks up his sleeve. I think he's far more dangerous, especially when he's cornered."

"I don't want you fighting my battles." Carol sighed but

didn't say more. If she was truly certain she could deal with this on her own, she'd have been far more assertive in her response to Terrance.

"I promise not to sucker punch anyone." Terrance stepped back and picked up his bag. "That's the best I can do at the moment. Now I'm going to go check on the status of the contract Marta is going to sign."

"What would I do without you?" Carol blinked slowly and smiled earnestly. "Maybe I should start using you for all sorts of things I'm avoiding. You want to clean out the attic at my parents' estate before next week?"

"I saw the letter." Terrance laughed. "The downside of opening your mail is having to put the really urgent stuff I know you don't want to read right on top. The lawyer has been sending you those letters for over a year. But it sounds like this is finally it. You need to get the place cleaned out."

"The buyer has been patient," Carol hummed. "But apparently that's run out."

"I can find a company to box everything up and have it moved to a storage unit or something. It's not as if you need to be up there digging through the family heirlooms."

"That's the thing," Carol rubbed at her temple. "I think I want to do that. Want is a strong word. I think I should do it myself. My mother has been gone more than a year now and I've avoided anything and everything that had to do with her. If I move all that stuff into storage, it'll still be hanging over my head. I need to face it once and for all."

"Maybe take a friend," Terrance suggested. "You're

probably right that it's time to do something about it, but you don't need to do it alone."

"No wonder Marta is already falling for you. You walk around looking like that," she said waving her hand at him. "And spouting insightful little nuggets of wisdom."

"She is not falling for me. Marta doesn't strike me as the kind of girl who falls for anyone. With her, I imagine it's more of a tiptoeing into the unknown with a flashlight in one hand and her other fist swinging."

"That's perfect. You know how to take a punch."

"We shouldn't even joke about this," Terrance let his face fall serious. "Marta is a cornerstone in what you are trying to build. The situation is incredibly delicate, and I certainly don't want to be the reason it falls apart. She's a special woman, but my loyalty is here with the company and your strategy."

Carol rolled her eyes. "That's horribly boring and probably stupid."

"Probably?" Terrance asked.

"Putting a shot at happiness behind business prospects as far as priorities go, can't possibly be a good idea. But since it's what I've done my entire life, I'm really in no position to say for sure. I wouldn't use what I've done as a roadmap toward anything."

"You have an amazing life," Terrance interjected quickly. "And you're changing other people's lives for the better too. If you wanted anything else badly enough, you'd have had it by now. The right thing must not have come along yet."

Carol looked at the framed photograph of her parents she kept on a bookshelf by her desk. One of the few personal effects in her office. Her mother's stern stare bored through her. "Or maybe I didn't settle down because I knew how badly my mother wanted me to."

"That's a pretty serious commitment to rebellion." Terrance chuckled. "And if that's the case, I think you can let it go now that she's gone. I'm sure she'd understand."

"You can't imagine how badly she wanted me to marry. My entire existence after the age of fifteen was dedicated to the goal of finding me a husband. Every interaction, every event I attended was like me casting a line and desperately hoping my bait was enough. And when it wasn't, my mother decided it was because I had made some kind of mistake. There was hell to pay."

Carol had only rarely spoken of her childhood, and when she had it was always vague. Something had shifted between them lately. Carol and Terrance bonded early on, loyal to one another. Rooting for success and working hard in tandem. There were, however, lines they didn't cross. Conversations they didn't engage in. The introduction of Marta into their lives opened new doors, blurring the lines.

Terrance welcomed it. Like any new territory, he was ready to explore. Carol was his boss, someone he cared about, and he wanted to see her thrive. But there was also the desire to know what made her tick. How did a woman with her ambition also balance endless compassion for others? There were questions over the years he'd almost asked, and now it seemed he might soon have the chance.

"Was there anyone you almost married?" Terrance asked, sliding his bag off his shoulder and taking a seat across from her. There was plenty to do, other places to be but she seemed eager to get some of this off her chest.

"Myron Salyers." Carol closed her eyes and painted on a dreamy expression. "We were engaged. My mother pulled a lot of strings to make that happen."

"And you cut them all?"

Carol laughed, but her eyes looked sad. "Basically. I was about as close to a runaway bride as you can be without actually making it to the church. My mother never forgave me for it."

"I'm sure Myron wasn't too pleased either."

"Actually," Carol snorted and covered her eyes, "he was relieved. About a year later, I ran into him and his boyfriend on a beach in Miami. The three of us had a great laugh about the lengths our parents were willing to go to marry us off."

"He was gay and he was going to marry you just because his mother wanted that?" Terrance shook his head in disbelief. "What kind of parents were these? It sounds more like the mob."

"I think there would be some definite overlap on a Venn diagram. Myron was so happy I called it off. Times were different back then. He didn't exactly get to be his true self. But he moved away, dodged his mother's future attempts, and built a life he was proud of. He died a few years ago in a car accident and I thought about how bad it would have been if we went through with the marriage and he didn't get to live the best life he could."

Terrance took in the story and tried to imagine what that pressure would have been like. "I'm starting to understand why you rebelled so long."

"But what did I rob myself of?" Carol raised her brows and leaned back in her chair. "Hell, don't listen to me. I'm being dramatic. It's not easy when your mom is your villain."

"I bet," Terrance tried. He didn't want his face to fall or his body language to change.

"Oh, what an idiot I am. I'm sorry. I know you didn't have the chance to even know your mother. I'm over here complaining about mine who lived to the ripe old age of ninety-six."

"Don't apologize," Terrance insisted. "My mother is a mystery to me. Maybe I'm the lucky one. The unknown is sort of a gift."

"And also not," Carol said somberly. "I know you had a wonderful aunt and uncle who raised you. I do wish you knew more about your parents."

"I could have," Terrance admitted. "I think if I'd have asked, someone would have said more. The only thing I know is that I was dropped off at daycare in the morning and never picked up."

"I am certain there must have been some unbearable circumstances that led to that. Nothing you did would have changed anything. I'm sorry if I was being insensitive, complaining about my mother."

"She sounds sort of awful," Terrance replied. "So I don't mind at all."

"Awful is being generous. But I am a grown woman. She's gone. I can't let it keep shaping my life."

"Which is why," Terrance said, grinning wryly, "if there happened to be a man who seemed perfect for you, you wouldn't hesitate. Even if he was a member of the board?"

Carol rolled her eyes but seemed only playfully annoyed. "He's off-limits. It would be a real conflict of interest if I even considered anything like that."

"At some point," Terrance pressed, "you've got to stop letting the rest of the world tell you what you can and can't have. Especially when you deserve everything."

Carol tipped her head back and looked up at the ceiling of her office. "Messy. All of this is messy. You and I should be focused on the goal, not all this. Wouldn't life be easier if you could just turn off the emotions?"

"Maybe," Terrance acquiesced. "But would it be worth living?"

"We're playing with fire." Carol didn't go as far as to name their potential dangers. She didn't suggest that Terrance dating Marta would be disastrous. Or that Carol being interested in Robert would be trouble. It was implied.

"Oh Carol," Terrance replied playfully, "we're fireproof."

5

Carol

Seeing Nancy twice in such a short period of time was odd. Their last dinner ended with Eli making a scene like an angry toddler. Carol had been evaluating her boundaries lately. Those very intentional barriers she set up between her and the world. So many of them had been about self-preservation. About combatting the way she'd grown up and the constant pressure her mother put on her. The distance she'd laid between herself and Nancy was mostly based on how their lives had diverged. The different paths they took. After having dinner together, even if it was rudely interrupted by Eli, something had clicked. A reminder that while they might have taken different paths, something had bonded them years ago.

"You really didn't have to do this with me," Carol sighed. She was standing on the bottom step of her mother and father's estate. A large brick set of steps that led to an impressively ornate front door.

"Are you kidding me," Nancy chuckled. "I am dying to find out what your parents kept locked away in that attic. Is it going to be bodies? Affairs? You know there is something juicy up there." Nancy's earrings were bright red and dangled from her petite ears. She had a casual shirt with handprints of her grandchildren painted across the front. She was the apotome of ease and joy. Clearly a fun grandma.

"Don't get your hopes up," Carol warned. "My mother wasn't exciting enough for any of those things. Her full-time job was to nag me about all the things I was doing wrong."

Nancy's bubbly exuberance deflated. "I always hated that for you. The first few times I met your mother, I thought she was just lovely."

"As most people did," Carol groaned. That was the hard part about the complicated feelings she had for her mother. Francine knew how to make a good impression. She didn't rear her ugly side in mixed company. So when Carol wanted to complain to a friend, it always felt like she was just being dramatic. Nancy, however, had been understanding, giving Carol the benefit of the doubt. And she'd hung around enough to get glimpses of the nasty side of Francine.

"Thank you for believing me when I told you about my mother. So many people assumed I was crazy. I'd tell them about how vindictive and cruel she could be, and they'd defend her based on their brief meetings with her. It would be so deflating."

"I'll admit I nearly fell for that," Nancy explained as they both made their way in through the front door. The marble floor was pristine and the smell of fresh flowers greeted them. "But I saw through her the first time she tried to get me to pressure you into some part of her agenda. I think I was supposed to get you to go on a double date with me and Leon. She had a few men in mind for you and I was supposed to pull some strings and convince you it was just serendipity. It was quite an elaborate ruse. In that moment, I knew her intentions were not coming from a positive place."

"I've been wrestling with the idea that maybe I stayed single all these years, chased off all the men in my life, just to spite her." Carol stood, frozen in the entryway of her childhood home. It felt dangerous to have this conversation in a house that held so many memories of her mother. The walls and her mother's essence seemed intertwined. Not in an earthy "branches grown together" type way. More parasitic. It was impossible to divorce her mother from this house. That's why she was selling it.

The house was quiet, though it was obviously not empty. Empty houses collect dust and cobwebs. They smell of stale air. The staff here, dwindled down to two, worked every day as if they were still running a busy household. The skills they honed for cleaning and the upkeep of the house were only surpassed by their ability to fade into the shadows at the sound of Carol's arrival. It had become this quiet agreement between them all. Carol was endlessly grateful for their loyal service and ensured they were well paid. But along the way, over the year since her mother died, they'd begun to realize that chit-chat in the drafty halls of this too-large estate was unpleasant.

The staff was busy and focused. Carol was normally using all her mental capacity to rein in the tidal wave of emotions that came with entering the house. So they all let each other off the hook and steered clear.

Carol had arranged the time today to clean out the attic. The stairs leading to it had been swept. Boxes that had lingered there for a while had been moved. The bulbs lighting the way up the normally dim hallway looked recently replaced. Like a car driving closely behind a snow-plow, the path for her was freshly cleared. Smooth sailing. The luxury that always came with her place in society. One she never took for granted.

Peeking her head into the long-forgotten space, Carol searched for the light switch. She ran her hand flush against the wall until she finally felt it. Flipping it on revealed something far more daunting than Carol imagined.

"There is so much crap up here," Nancy gasped. "Did you know all this was up here?"

Carol shook her head. "I haven't been up here in ages. Probably since I was a kid. I had no idea they'd accumulated so many things." Carol laughed. "I can hear my mother commenting on how I never accumulated a family."

"Tune her ghost ass out," Nancy insisted. "I met plenty of those men you're talking about, and I don't think your mother was the problem. You deserve someone who can appreciate you as a strong, accomplished woman. None of those men stacked up. You didn't throw your life away just to get back at your mom. You held to your convictions. I can't tell you how many of my friends, women our age, are finally dealing with the fact that they compromised it all for a man they settled for. And that man is now leaving them for a younger woman. Weak-minded bastards are not worth giving up your passion and drive for."

"You always know what to say." Carol sighed, taking a look at the racks of clothes hanging against the far wall. "If my mother were a ghost, this is where she'd be. Guarding all her precious clothes."

"Should we take a stroll down memory lane?" Nancy asked, half playful, half compassionate. "I know these things aren't easy. When I lost my father and we had to go through all his things, it was emotional. No matter what type of relationship you had, it's hard."

Carol flipped the lid of the closest leather chest open. "Oh no," she hummed, stepping back abruptly. "Why is this the first one I opened?"

"What is it?" Nancy asked, anxiously reaching in and pulling out one of the ten or so leather-bound books. She flipped the pages quickly against her thumb.

"My mother's journals. I had a feeling they were up here, but I never had the courage to look at them."

"Because you shouldn't." Nancy tossed the journal back in the leather chest as if it might suddenly bite her. "These are the inner thoughts of an unstable woman. You were far too often the recipient of her dysfunction. That's all you can expect to find on those pages. Probably far worse than the things she said out loud to you. And those were bad enough."

"Or," Carol interjected, wanting to reach for the books, "maybe it's all the positive things she couldn't bring herself to say. Or guilt for how she treated me."

"That's not worth the gamble." Nancy put her hand over the closed chest. "You just said I give good advice. Trust me. If you go down that rabbit hole, you won't come back out. And she's gone. You won't be able to ask for clarification, or yell at her, or forgive her."

"So I should just go through these boxes of old Christmas decorations and photo albums and forget all about those books?"

"Exactly." Nancy moved to a tower of old magazines. "Look at these. I read every one of these when I was a girl. Remember the quizzes? I was obsessed."

"My mother hated that I read these. Teen magazines were trash in her opinion. She wanted me to read Debutante Journal."

"But she kept these," Nancy said, pulling a small stack into her lap as she settled onto an old rocking chair. "So many heartthrobs."

"My father kept these," Carol said, her breath catching in her throat. "Look. He wrote a note to the staff." Seeing her father's handwriting was a blast from the past. She could recall perfectly where on his desk he kept this particular notepad.

Nancy cooed as she read the note. "Carol's prize possessions. Store safely."

Carol blinked her tears away. "I don't know how he put up with her, or why. He was such a good man."

"That generation just held on for dear life. Marriage was an agreement and once you were in, there was no turning back."

"I think it put him in an early grave." Carol hugged the note to her chest for a second before putting it back on a stack of magazines. Nancy was a few pages in, already giggling.

"I suppose we're at a crossroads," she said, humming and rocking as she flipped another page. "We could dig through your mother's old hat collection. Catalog your father's business papers. Or we could take this quiz about what kind of princess we would be."

Carol glanced around the attic. Her mother's dresses loomed like judgmental apparitions. "You know I'm a diva princess. And you'd be a rebel heiress." Carol plucked a magazine from the stack and pulled over an antique chair covered in dust. It would smudge terribly on her crisp, snow-white pants. There was something alluring about messing up her expensive wardrobe. Just like she had as a child. But now her mother would not be there to scold her.

6

Marta – Fourteen

The cracks in the glass of her family had shattered. They were all shards, strewn around and ready to cut anyone who got too close. Losing Jonah had broken it. The last straw. Her mother embraced alcohol the way some might a soldier returning from war. There was a desperation. A grasping and gripping as if holding on for dear life. The drinking seemed to help in some ways. There were fewer over-the-top public arguments. Those took too much planning and perseverance to pull off. Those outbursts were replaced by drunken public gallivanting. Still embarrassing, but most of the time, quieter.

Her mother had turned into a quitter of all things besides the booze. She quit being a parent. The few things she could have been counted on to do before Jonah's death were finished now. No food shopping. No laundromat. During the day, her door was closed. Lights off. Her third shift job as a housekeeper in a hotel laundry room suited her parenting style perfectly. It gave her the perfect excuse to disengage.

Glenn was the parent now. He'd just turned twenty, yet he found ways to make it all work. Technically he lived at home with his mother and Marta, but he was rarely there. He made sure they had food and fought endlessly with Wendy about her drinking problem. Some days it was easier when he was gone. Marta had found small ways to keep her mother still and while Glenn meant well, he usually stirred things up and left.

Vocational school had given him some skills and a few morsels of hope to hang on to. A local mechanic shop hired him and gave him about as many hours as he could handle. With raw, oil-stained fingers, Glenn would sign Marta's failed math quizzes and field trip permission slips. He doled out pep talks about friendship drama and warned her about the world.

The lines that blurred between them made for dangerous territory. A brother giving astute advice wasn't unheard of. But having to teach his sister everything a young girl needed to know proved awkward and sometimes unproductive. He'd bought her a box of maxi pads when she got her first period. Showed her how to shave her legs, though he'd mostly been wrong about the technique. Now as he tried to usher her safely into adulthood, they'd begun to butt heads. Just like any teenager fighting back against authority, Marta didn't want to hear his advice or heed his warnings. So more and more, he stayed away.

Walking home from the bus, a cold rain drenching her, she was relieved to see the blue truck pull up by her. It wasn't Glenn, but a friend of his. A kid who'd graduated a year or two after Glenn but grew up only a few streets over.

"Hey kid, you'll freeze. Hop in." Eddy leaned over and lifted the lock on the passenger side.

"Thanks," Marta breathed, blinking the falling rain out of her eyes as she rounded the front of the truck. She had a two-mile walk ahead of her. But that was her own fault. Detention, long block, the one that lasted an hour and a half, meant there was no bus to ride home. "I missed the bus."

"More like you got busted and had long block," Eddy laughed. "Trust me I walked this route this time of day plenty when I was your age. What'd you do?"

"Mrs. Bloyster hates me," Marta groaned, pulling her wet backpack onto her lap and closing the truck door. "All I did was disagree with her and she gave me long block detention."

"Disagree? About what?" Eddy's hair was long, messy, and fell slightly over his sharp blue eyes. She'd noticed before the way his jaw set. She liked it. Boxy and strong. The way he squinted when he laughed always intrigued her. His cologne was one she'd smelled in a bottle at the mall before. A new-looking tattoo adorned his forearm. Eddy was a cool guy. He'd been that way in school, but now he had a job at a motorcycle shop in town and that upped his status even higher in Marta's opinion. More than that, he was nice. Always looking out for Marta when he could.

"She was going on and on about Romeo and Juliet and their epic love story. I said they were two stupid kids who were codependent and dramatic. I swear I will never love a guy so much that I'd die over it. How stupid."

"Oh, she must have gotten all red in her round face with that." Eddy laughed and slapped his hand to the steering wheel. Something stirred in Marta. She'd wielded a bit of power, making an older and much cooler guy laugh. It was intoxicating.

"I thought her head would explode," Marta went on. "She tried to say that the intensity it's written with is meant to be dramatic. Then I asked why she condones suicide and she kicked me out."

"Epic," Eddy said, with a wry smile. "I didn't know you had it in you. You're always so quiet. Marta, bad to the bone. I guess you're not a little kid anymore."

If there were a higher compliment, she hadn't heard one. "I'm not a kid," she agreed hastily. "I'm fourteen. I'll be fifteen in three weeks."

"Damn," Eddy said. He nodded as if this was impressive. "I guess I didn't realize that. Yeah, you are older than I thought."

"You're only eighteen," she reminded him. "You're not much older than I am." She watched his face intently as he drove, rain pelting the windshield.

"You're right." His agreement made her heart soar. "It's really coming down," he said, flipping the defroster on, the vents taking aim at the foggy windows. "I better clear these up before I get you home and your brother thinks we were in here fogging them up."

She laughed, but she wasn't entirely certain what they might be doing to cause the windows to fog. "Glenn isn't home. He never is anymore. And, my brother is not my keeper," she said, trying to sound as mature as possible. "He likes to think he is."

"Oh, he just cares about you. No offense, but your parents are so jacked up. I think it's good you have him."

Her cheeks pinked and she looked away too quickly to be casual.

"Hey, I didn't mean anything by it." He leaned over and slapped his hand to her knee, trying to draw her attention back. "Don't take it the wrong way. We don't get to pick who our parents are."

She knew he was talking, but all her energy went to the hand on her leg. The heat of his palm on her wet jeans. The way he squeezed just a bit before letting go. "Glenn doesn't get to decide what I do, and neither do my parents," Marta said, straightening her back and trying to look bigger than she was.

"That's cool," Eddy said, casually shrugging. "I like that you take care of yourself. You're not like other kids your age, that's for sure. Every time I see you out, you look like you've got everything handled."

Sweaty palms and a thudding heart, Marta devoured his words. She felt as though she'd been waiting ages for someone to notice how different she was from all the other girls in her grade. Not obsessed with the latest hairstyle or boy band, Marta understood how useless those things were. "I do have things handled."

"I guess you've had to figure things out for yourself really. I remember when I heard about Jonah. Things were already pretty messed up for you guys and then that happened."

"Yeah," Marta croaked out. She righted herself and tried to imagine what a grown woman might say. "That's why I don't bother with kid stuff. The girls in my grade are obsessed with the stupidest things. They don't know what the world is really like." She'd never taken gymnastics but she'd watched the Olympics. That felt like a backflip off the balance beam with a perfectly stuck landing. If it wasn't immature, she'd be pumping her fists in the air.

"But then you don't get to be a kid. Trust me, I've got a job and car insurance. I miss being your age."

"You wouldn't if you had my life." Marta didn't mean to sound like she wanted pity. Her mother was addicted to being a victim, and she tried really hard to never come across that way.

"If you ever need a ride, just call me. I don't like you walking home alone, even when it's not raining. I know the kids that go to your school. Especially the boys. They are always looking for a beautiful girl like you somewhere out on your own."

Her toes tingled and her throat closed up. No one had ever called her beautiful before. Especially not someone like Eddy. "I'm not worried about them." She shifted in her seat.

"So, you won't call me for a ride? I go by here this time of day pretty often. And I bet you've got long block a lot too."

She giggled, an unfamiliar ultra-feminine little laugh. "Sometimes."

"Then I'll look for you when I go by."

"Okay." She pulled her bag closer as they approached the driveway of her apartment. "You can drop me here."

Eddy had been by their place before. He'd seen the crappy car in the driveway and the unkempt yard. But she felt suddenly self-conscious.

"You don't have to do that with me," Eddy said, a sideways glance passing between them.

"Do what?" She gulped.

"I've known your family a long time. I don't need to drop you off at the corner. You don't have to pretend with me."

She didn't reply, instead she just nodded and offered a small, grateful smile. That faded instantly when she saw her mother. Her robe was open, a barely-there lace nightgown soaked from the rain.

"No," Marta gasped. Her face burned with anger and embarrassment. "I'm so sorry." As she reached for the car door handle, Eddy touched her arm gently.

"Don't get out." His voice was a raspy whisper. "I can take you somewhere else. Want to go to your dad's?"

Thinking of her father's dark, nearly empty apartment didn't bring her much comfort. He was working double shifts and the fridge would be empty. She was only allowed to visit on court-ordered days of the week and this wasn't one of them. Going there now would be like launching a rocket and just waiting for it to fall back to the earth and destroy everything.

"I can't go there. It's not his day to have me and she'll make a scene. I don't want to go back to court."

"Then I'll take you somewhere else. She's not your problem." He politely kept his eyes off of Wendy Leduc and her drenched see-through nightgown.

"She's drunk," Marta explained, in case somehow that wasn't obvious. "I can't leave her out in the rain."

Eddy breathed out a humorless laugh through his nose. "Is that what you've been told?" He put the truck in reverse and his arm went behind her as he turned to see out the back window. His tires screeched a bit as he blew out of the driveway and back onto the street. "You can leave her. She's an adult. If she wants to get drunk and stand in the rain, that's her problem."

"But I can get her back in the house."

"She can get herself back in the house. Or she won't. You're not the parent."

Marta gulped and licked her dry lips. "Where are we going?"

"To hang," Eddy explained. "You can hang with me until your brother gets out of work. Let him deal with her."

"He hardly does anymore. He's working a ton and he doesn't really sleep at home." Her eyes were wet with tears but she fought them away. "Really, it's no big deal. I can go home."

"And leave me hanging?" Eddy asked, pretending to sound hurt. "A bunch of buddies and I were going to Murphy's to play pool. Come hang, have a basket of fries. Your mom will be passed out and you can have some peace and quiet when you get home."

"Okay," Marta sniffled. "I don't have any money with me though. It's back at the house."

"My treat," Eddy insisted. "Your brother has fixed my dad's car for hardly any money for a couple years now. It's the least I can do."

Marta wanted to know what this was. Why he was bothering to help her. Pity? A debt paid? Attraction?

On some level, that didn't matter. No one like Eddy had ever swept in and told her she could leave. Everyone always reminded Marta of what her mother had lost, how hard her life had been. How someone had to hold her together. The permission to walk away, the attention of someone like Eddy, was a mind-altering jolt. What she didn't know then was the shell game she was playing. An illusion. Changing one problem for another. Like trying to mend a broken leg with a sledgehammer. In the end, everything gets smashed.

7

Marta

The rev of a motorcycle made her jump. She'd decided after leaving her mother's house that it would be better to just check into the hotel. Carol had insisted on covering her travel expenses even though she was back in her hometown. There were probably some cousins who didn't hate her who would have let her stay. But the anonymity of the hotel was too alluring.

When the motorcycle engine cut out, she realized it had pulled up beside her. The familiar blue eyes were dancing with excitement. "I thought that was you," Eddy said, dropping the kickstand and hopping quickly off his bike. "Your brother said you were coming back to town soon. I had to pick up some parts in the city. He said you'd be staying here. I saw you out of the corner of my eye and had to pull over."

"Eddy. How are you?" Marta opened her arms for a hug and he was lifting her off her feet and spinning her around before she could catch her breath.

"You moving back here or what?" Eddy's cologne was the same and it teleported her back to their days together.

"Just visiting." She rolled her eyes. "Reluctantly visiting. It's work stuff. But how are you? You still at the bike shop?"

"Always," Eddy said with a big smile. "I run it now. That gives me time to make my own schedule and be out riding in the middle of the day."

"Nice," Marta complimented. "I just came from my mom's house." It was probably an unimportant detail to anyone else, but she knew Eddy would grasp the context.

"Damn, sorry to hear that. I see her every now and then around town. She flips me off."

"No she doesn't," Marta said, covering her blushing cheeks. "I hope you're kidding."

"I'm not. She hates me. She has since you and I dated. Apparently, she forgets all the crazy crap she did to you. I'm the bad guy for dating you."

"I hate that you had to deal with her and Glenn. I wish they understood that you were just helping me. I don't honestly know what I'd have done without you."

"You'd have done fine," Eddy offered kindly. "You always knew how to take care of yourself. I just came along when you needed a break. I caught some hell for it, but it was worth it."

"You were a saint," Marta said, remembering what it had felt like to find refuge from her life in Eddy's arms. Falling for him, her first love, was heady and looking back she'd probably made it all more dramatic than it needed to be.

"I was far from a saint. Now, looking back, I really had no business dating a fifteen-year-old. It kind of haunts me."

"We didn't date until I was sixteen and you were always completely respectful and never pressured me into anything. You were really great to me."

"Oh girl, we remember things pretty differently. We should have a coffee sometime and sort it out."

"How about now?" Marta gestured to the hotel. "I'm staying here for a few days. They've got a great coffee bar in the lobby."

"Now?" Eddy asked, looking doubtful. "You're going to drop everything and have a coffee with your old boyfriend?"

"Before you were my boyfriend, you were my friend. And to be honest, I'm kind of in this weird place with what I'm doing for work. I'd love to get your opinion on some stuff. You know me better than almost anyone."

"I doubt that. You've certainly changed over the years. The girl I knew wouldn't have the cash to stay in this hotel."

"A few things have changed, but not the stuff you knew. Maybe I wish I had changed all those things, but I can't seem to. Do you have time for coffee?"

"I've got loads of time," Eddy said, gesturing with one hand toward the hotel and putting the other on the small of her back. It felt a little like falling through time. Being a teenager again. For all the angst and pain, there was still something redeeming about being young. And Eddy reminded her of those days.

When they were settled in a little booth in the hotel lobby coffee shop, Marta explored Eddy's face with more scrutiny. This was the first person she'd kissed. The person she'd cried with when she finally allowed herself the grace to do so. Her protector. Her savior. Yet it had all fallen apart eventually.

"Don't look at me like that," Eddy begged. "Seriously, my heart can't take that."

"Like what?"

"The way you used to look at me. It was like pumping my ego with helium. I'd just float off. I was weak."

Marta stirred sugar into her coffee and furrowed her brows. "You make it sound like I seduced you."

"No," Eddy waved his hands. "Not at all. You were just so helpless and you'd look at me like . . ." He trailed off, seeming unsure.

"Like you were my everything." Marta surprised herself with the candor. Seeing Eddy again, especially after the disastrous encounter with her mother seemed very full circle. "Sorry, that's cheesy but it's true. You were really good to me."

"Marta, I could have been good to you and not dated

you. You're giving me too much credit. I got between you and your brother."

"No," Marta rushed the word out and touched his arm. "Glenn and I were already on shaky ground. It's not easy doing what he did. Trying to parent a sibling. I wasn't listening to him."

"But I could have helped with that. Instead, I pitted you against him. You had to basically choose between us. If you'd have just met a guy at school and had a normal relationship, maybe you could have weathered it better."

"I hate that you've spent all this time thinking about it that way. I couldn't just meet a kid at school. I needed you. I needed someone who could pick me up when my mom was losing it. Someone who had a job and could make sure I didn't go too long without eating. You saw how bad it was and I could cry with you. More importantly, the reason I needed you and not someone else was because you were the first person to give me permission to take some control of my life. You were the person I needed at that time." The tears were streaming freely down her face. Apparently Eddy had that effect on her.

He closed his eyes and tipped his head back. "You were strong. I hated to see what was happening to you. I was always a sucker for tears."

Marta wiped her cheeks and drew in a deep breath. It was painful but she had to ask. "Did you love me?"

The few beats of hesitation stung. "I did love you. I don't know what kind of love it was. I wanted you to be okay. I wanted to save you. No one looked at me the way you did. But now I've got nieces and I think about what I'd do if some nineteen-year-old tried to date them when they were sixteen."

"I know your sister. She's a great person and basically a super mom. Your nieces are never going to need what I did."

"But it was a need, Marta. I don't know if you'd have loved me if you hadn't needed me so much."

"Oh," Marta covered her eyes. "You don't understand. You are the only healthy, good relationship I've ever been in. You treated me well and you cared about me. Don't tell me I had it all wrong."

"I did care about you. But I was an idiot kid. I didn't treat you quite as well as you think. And it scares me if my nineteen-year-old loser self is the bar you have for a good relationship. Not being a jerk is not good enough. I put you in risky situations. I took you around a lot of older people. A lot of drugs and drinking."

"But I never did that stuff. You never pressured me to."

"Do you know why I broke up with you, Marta?" His pained expression needled at her heart as she tried to deliver the right answer.

"You were working a lot more. Then your grandfather was sick. You just had too much going on."

"We'd been dating more than a year. I was partying a lot. I was going to cheat on you. I knew it. I hadn't yet, but I was going to. I looked at you one night and I realized that someday you were going to be this whole person. You wouldn't be stuck with your parents and their drama forever.

I didn't know when it would happen, but you'd be okay someday and I didn't want you to wake up next to me when it happened."

"It hasn't happened. I wouldn't say I'm okay."

"I think you're doing pretty damn good."

"Staying with you wouldn't have been some kind of burden. If you only knew the terrible choices I made after, you might have reconsidered."

"I was not the guy for you. I wanted to be. But I knew I wasn't. It was one of the hardest things I've ever had to do. I hated to break up with you. It killed me to hear you married Keith. I never liked him. I knew he wasn't good enough for you. Then so much stuff went down with your dad dying and the way people blamed you. I know it got ugly. I wanted to go to his funeral, but I didn't want to make it any harder for you."

"It was a bumpy time after my father died. And yeah, Keith was a whole other story. He was not good," Marta admitted.

"One of my friends, Talia, she dated him before you. He wasn't good to her either. I wanted to say something. But it's only in the movies where someone stands up and objects at the wedding."

"I wish you had. I'd have jumped on the back of your motorcycle and never looked back." She dropped her head and sipped her coffee. "Sorry. I'm not trying to rewrite history. I just can't believe all these years we've been looking at it so differently. When I think about you, I'm always grateful. When you think about me you feel guilty."

"I guess maybe it's somewhere in the middle. It is good to know you don't resent me or blame me for anything. I really did love you."

"I loved you too." Marta dabbed at the corners of her eyes. "Please don't feel bad for being my first everything. You pulled up that day in your truck in the rain. What you didn't know is I'd have gotten in any car with anyone going anywhere but home. Thank God it was you. Thank God you took such good care of me."

Eddy nodded bashfully and an ease seemed to spread across his face. "I'm glad we ran into each other today. I've always wanted to check in with you. Once you left town, I figured I'd never see you again. You'd be on to your second husband, starting a family."

"I haven't dated anyone really since I left Keith. I don't trust myself anymore. I don't know what I'm supposed to expect out of people. And this conversation certainly furthers that concern." Shaking her head at the state of things, she caught a glimpse of his sweet smile.

"I'm sure you'll figure it out. But if I am the bar you're measuring it off of, scrap that. Move it way up." He motioned animatedly.

"I'm sure whoever you're with now would disagree."

"Actually, my ex would give you a list of reasons I'm right. Lots of socks right next to the hamper and too much time at the shop. But it was a pretty amicable break-up really."

The realization that they were both single seemed to hang between them. Looming like smoke in a cigar room.

Her words waved it away. "Well, I doubt we'll both be unlucky in love forever."

"Cheers to that," he said, raising his mug and clinking it against hers. "How long are you in town?"

"I don't know. How long do you think it would take my entire family to somehow become presentable enough to be featured on a national platform and speak highly of me?"

"So, you're moving back forever?" He laughed. "Why in the world do you need your family to do that?"

"I've been given an award and it'll change everything. I'll have a career. Doors will open for me. But the catch is, they'll expect to know me."

"And knowing you means knowing all the things that happened to you?"

"Exactly. A lot of people around here don't like me. They loved my dad and they have this impression of what happened when he died. Then my mother is obviously a detractor. Can you imagine these people going back to school and talking to my teachers? They wouldn't be able to come up with one redeeming story about me. So I have this enormous contract I'm supposed to sign, and I came back here to try to find some way to make it work."

"Maybe you're overthinking it?" Eddy asked, hardly sure of it himself. "What happens if you sign the contract and let the rest just happen? If your mom is a mess and people in town talk trash; will it really matter?"

"I thought about that. But I'm not the traditional recipient of this award. I'm representing something bigger than myself. And I have a feeling I won't be representing it too well."

For the third time this afternoon, Terrance sent her a text. She hadn't replied yet. And now when her phone chirped, she slipped it into her bag.

"Let me help," Eddy said, sitting up a little straighter.

"I guess you haven't shaken that knight in shining armor thing yet."

"Maybe it's penance." He grimaced, the guilt still clearly gnawing at him. "Your uncle Lin is the one who really has it out for you, right?"

"I know you weren't at my father's funeral, but I suppose you heard that he called me a murderer in the middle of the eulogy."

"I might have heard some rumbles about it. But I never gave it any credence. I spent plenty of time with you and your father. For some reason, he didn't hate me."

"He liked you," Marta corrected.

"Why? Usually, a dad doesn't want his daughter dating someone older. A guy with a motorcycle."

"That's what made my dad so strange. He had all these rules and hang-ups. He expected us to be so many different types of things. But he also wanted us to be happy, and he trusted us when we said we were. Nothing else mattered when it came to that."

"He was one of a kind," Eddy replied somberly. "And you were good to him. Better than anyone saw. There were a lot of things about the guy I didn't understand, but I never doubted how much you loved him. When I heard people giving you crap after he died, I knew it was all garbage."

"I appreciate that. But almost no one would agree with you. I might need more than one person on my side here in town."

"Well, let me help with your uncle. I work on all his bikes. Have for years. Lin is mostly just a hard ass but he listens to me. I bet I can get him to understand why, at a minimum, he should just keep his mouth shut about how he feels."

"My family has never really been good at that." She rubbed her hand across her brow. "Uncle Lin was always my favorite. That's what makes it tough. He and my dad were best friends. Dysfunctional for sure, but they loved each other. As far as he's concerned, he lost his best friend because of me."

"Let me see what I can do," Eddy promised, reaching across and touching her hand. "That'll make us even for anything I've been feeling bad about all these years."

"Deal. Then we'll have a clean slate." She nearly said fresh start but that sounded presumptuous and not really what she was looking for. As good as it was to sit with Eddy and sink back into that feeling of new love and safety she'd once felt with him, a lot had changed. If things in her life worked out, a hell of a lot more was about to change too. It wouldn't be the time to look backward.

In a flash of fantasy, she imagined what it might be like to rip up the contract in her bag and jump on the back of Eddy's bike. His place was out on the edge of town on a quiet wooded property. She could write under a pen name and sell her books to small publishing houses for just enough cash to get by. She wouldn't have to explain anything to Eddy. He knew her. He understood that she'd loved her father, even when things went bad in the end. He didn't question why she listened to the same album over and over. It wasn't just the love of the songs but the space they took in her mind. The lyrics fought like an army against more intrusive thoughts she wasn't ready to deal with.

Eddy knew quiet wasn't her friend and sitting still didn't suit her. Marta needed perpetual movement. Centripetal force to keep all of her in the bucket that was spinning over and over. If she stopped, she'd spill out everywhere.

The idea of being with someone who already understood the hardest-to-explain parts of herself was appealing.

"I hope you stay around a little while," Eddy said, his eyes twinkling. "I'd like to hear more about this award and your book. I bought a copy, but you know I don't really read much. My sister said it was real good."

"Tell her thanks," Marta replied, watching her pretend life with Eddy cascade down in front of her. This was what made her different. How her mind worked. She could imagine details. Play pretend. "And thank you for offering to help out with my uncle. I hope he's receptive."

"I can be persuasive." Eddy winked and again she felt it warm her heart. "Remember how I used to talk bouncers into letting you into clubs even though you were too young?"

"I do."

"Just another thing I feel bad for now."

"I had some of the best nights of my life dancing in the club with you. For a little while I got to feel completely free. That's what I'm looking for now. Some freedom to actually have a life I want."

"Then let me talk to the bouncers," Eddy joked. "The people standing in the way. I'll see what I can do."

They chatted for another hour about old times before Eddy checked his watch and cursed. "I've got to get back to the shop before Donnie burns the place down. I'll call you soon."

"It was so good to see you," Marta said into his shoulder as they hugged and said their goodbyes. "Whether you talk to Lin or not, call me soon."

8

Terrance

Terrance wasn't the type to hound a woman. Under normal circumstances, if he texted and didn't hear back he'd have moved on. But this was somewhere between personal and business. He wanted to hear Marta's voice because it brought his mind right back to the kiss they shared. But he needed to hear from her so he could feel confident that nothing about their agreement had changed.

When she did finally call, he braced for bad news. "Hey, I thought you'd tossed your phone and run off somewhere by now."

"It's crossed my mind," Marta admitted. Her voice sounded small and tired. He regretted not going back east with her.

"How did things go with your mom?"

"You know when you're having a really bad day and everything is just going wrong? Then you're walking around your house and your clothes get stuck on a drawer knob or a door handle?"

He chuckled at the image.

"My mother is the human equivalent of that door handle. That last straw *are you kidding me* feeling."

"So no celebration of your accomplishment then?"

"She pretended she'd never heard of the award before even though we've watched the ceremony together multiple times. Then when my news became positive, she pretended to break a dish in the kitchen. Pretty standard stuff for her, but I'm out of practice."

"I should have come with you."

"An audience is usually seen as a challenge to my mother."

"But I could have helped you after. I'm worried."

"About what? Me not signing the contract?" There was a tiny hitch in her voice. An indication of something she clearly wasn't ready to say outright. Marta wanted to know if all of this was only about the desired outcome. Or if he actually cared about what happened to her.

"You don't deserve to have to confront all of this just because something good happened to you. I feel like someone objective needs to be there to whisper that in your ear every five minutes or so."

She laughed and he felt the pulse of a relief beat through him. "It might need to be more frequent than that."

"I'm going to come out there. I don't want you talking yourself out of something you deserve just because there are too many voices around you saying otherwise."

"You need to help Carol. She's got a guy mailing her dead rats and trying to overthrow her at the company. She needs you."

"Carol's number one priority is you. Helping you is helping her. I think an impartial person could really help you right now."

"And you're impartial?"

"You said it yourself, I care about what happens to Carol too. We'll work everything out the best we can there. It'll all turn out fine. But if you want to bail because you can't see a way forward, I can be there as a temperature gauge. Maybe you're right, and it won't work. But at least you wouldn't have to decide that completely on your own." Terrance thought of what it would mean to hop on a plane tonight. All the work he'd be leaving behind. But this truly was the lynchpin to Carol's future and, by extension, his own. If he were being honest, though, it was the urge to hold Marta and comfort her that had him calculating flight times.

Marta hesitated. "I don't know. It was one thing to go to where my real life is now. I've distanced myself from so much of this place. I've been back one day and I already feel like the past is swallowing me up. I'm questioning so much."

"Exactly. I'm not going to try to oversell you on how great everything is or sugarcoat what I think will happen. I'll be honest with you. No strings attached. The last thing I want is for all of this to implode down the road. I'm not going to let that happen. But I'm not going to let you run before we know for sure."

Again, there was a long beat of silence. "When could you get here?"

"In the morning. I'll take the red-eye."

"You don't have to get here that quick."

"Where are you going in the morning? Back to see your mom?"

"No, I'm going to let her cool off for a day. I'm going to my old school. I'm hoping to find a teacher who didn't hate me and might be happy for me."

"Am I going to get to see pictures of you in old yearbooks? Because then it's well worth the red-eye flight."

"Don't make me change my mind."

"Okay, no old pictures. I'll be there."

"I'm glad." Marta sighed. "I can feel this place already affecting me. Maybe you're exactly what I need to stay sane. I don't really like who I am here. I don't like remembering who I was."

"I've met who you are now, and that's someone I'd gladly fly overnight to see."

"You might hear things about me. I've alluded to plenty but if you come here, you'll get it right from the source."

"You're the only source I care about. I believe you. Let everyone else talk and try to convince me you're anything other than great. It'll be a good test of what's to come." He knew his words could be perceived in different ways. What was to come to her and her career. What was to come between the two of them. He hoped she knew he was rooting for both. What he didn't want to have to do was choose. Because at this point, he had no idea, when push came to shove, where his loyalty would lie.

Carol had been endlessly supportive of him and his career. She yanked him up the corporate ladder and provided him with opportunities he'd have probably waited many more years for. And he liked her. She was a good person with a disproportionate number of faults compared to enemies. Not enough people wanted to see Carol succeed. That only fueled Terrance's loyalty to her. He'd been the underdog plenty in his life. People saw him and immediately made assumptions about who he was and what he did. Carol got a lot of the same treatment.

They'd become a team of two, mostly because no one else wanted to join their late night brainstorming and need for unrelenting honesty with each other. If no one else was in their corner then they owed that to each other. This would be no different. Terrance would fly out to Marta's hometown. Sink into the swamp of her past, and weigh in bluntly if it could be cleared up. If the slime and the stink and the muck Marta had warned about could be somehow filtered and fixed.

He didn't want to find out what he'd have to do if the answer was no. If Marta couldn't accept the award, Carol's entire career might be on the line. She'd staked everything on this working. But if Terrance helped move things forward and he was wrong, Marta would be destroyed in public and in her private life. There was a chance he'd lose one or both of them if he screwed this up. They were depending on his judgment, and the pressure was immense.

And none of that took into consideration just how much he wanted to hold Marta. To kiss her and protect her. There was danger in how much his feelings for her might skew his ability to be objective. Even knowing it, he couldn't seem to turn them off.

"I'll pick you up at the airport tomorrow," Marta said, sounding a bit more upbeat. "I'm exhausted. I'm going to swing by my brother's place with a bottle of wine and complain for a while about how awful my mother was. That should help."

"I'll text you my flight info when I get it. Sleep well. No matter what, you'll be okay."

"You sound so sure."

"You've made it this far. If that place and those people couldn't crush you when you were a kid, they're not going to now, knowing you're as strong as you are."

"I ran away. It was fight or flight, and I flew."

"Smart strategy at the time. You were alone. You aren't now. You have Carol and all her resources in your corner."

"And I have you," Marta said, her voice rising at the end.

"You do. And I'm a hell of a fighter."

9

Carol – Sixteen

It took over a month to plan her pitch. There was no begging at her house. Whining didn't get her anywhere with her parents. The only chance she really had was to formulate and deliver a concise argument and hope her father would be overwhelmed by the logic and her mother merciful enough to consider what she was saying.

Even the date had to be carefully selected. After studying the calendar, Carol had decided that today, the twenty-third of April would be best. Her mother had just had all her socialite friends over two days earlier. Carol had been her dutiful, impressive self. That would have her mother feeling warmly toward her. Plus it would mean her mother would have a whole month before having to meet with the group again.

That was key. Her mother wouldn't need to explain anything to them right away. And there wouldn't be a group of robot wives there to side with her and get her to change her mind. That's if Carol could convince her of what she wanted in the first place.

"Mother, are you busy?"

"I'm always busy," Francine reported curtly as she folded the letter she was writing and stuffed it into an envelope. After licking and sealing it she appraised her daughter closely. "But what is it?"

"Dad are you free to talk?" she asked, peeking over the top of her father's newspaper. He grinned, straightened his face quickly, and dropped the paper down to his lap.

"Of course. What do you need?"

"I wanted to talk to you both about the summer."

"What about it?" Francine asked, already sounding defensive.

"Mother, I've done everything you've asked of me over the years. Attended all the events, hopefully represented our family well."

Dallas chimed in. "You absolutely have. I'm very proud of all you've done. Your mother gave you direction and you followed it."

"I'm on track to be the valedictorian next year. I'm first in my class."

"Because your nose is always in a book," Francine hummed.

"Dear, she's balanced it all quite well actually. School, social events, and even service to the community. We're both very proud of you."

Francine huffed. "You do understand she's about to ask us for something, right? You're a smart man, tell me you can see that."

"Let's hear her out." Dallas gestured at his daughter, indicating the floor was hers.

Keeping her face steady and not gulping back the growing knot in her throat, Carol began to explain. "There is an internship at Sullivan Books this summer."

"Sullivan is a great company," Dallas commented, looking impressed. To Carol, her father's adoration was supreme, and it emboldened her to go on.

"I've been offered the position for the summer."

"You have commitments this summer," Francine reminded her. "The Olivers expect you to be their nanny again."

"I appreciate their confidence in me," Carol said, that line well-rehearsed in front of her mirror. "And I've enjoyed being able to care for their children over the last few summers. But I've made no commitment to them this year. They understood at the end of last year that I'd likely be taking on more of a professional role by this summer."

Francine scoffed. "Shall I buy you some suits like your father?"

"Don't tease, Francine," Dallas insisted. "Is it Preston over at Sullivan who's offered you the spot?"

"Yes," Carol said proudly. "He came to the school paper

three weeks ago, and after speaking with the editor and my teachers, he thought I would be perfect for the job."

"But why?" Francine asked, tossing her hands up. "Why spend your whole summer doing grunt work for no money? If you don't plan to nanny, there are many other things we could fill your summer with. The country club is always looking for young ladies to help host their larger events."

Carol bit back the words she wanted to say. That serving a bunch of men in a country club that's biggest selling point was the exclusion of anyone who didn't look like them was not her goal for the summer. "I'm sure that's a good opportunity too."

"Think of all the men you could meet there. Good men."

The country club's definition of what made a man good was drastically different, but Carol had learned long ago that debating her mother was pointless. "Well, you asked why I would want an internship at Sullivan Books. It would help immensely when I begin applying for colleges."

"Dear," Francine laughed, "you're not going to have any trouble getting into Fort Wright College. It's my alma mater, and you know how important I was there."

The religious women's college offered nothing Carol was looking for. The programs were limited, the restrictions were vast, and the message was not one she was looking for. "I plan to apply to multiple colleges. With my grades, an Ivy league school should be within reach."

Again her father beamed with pride. "Maybe you'll be a Yale girl. That's my alma mater, and while I didn't leave the indelible mark your mother did at her school, I could certainly put in a good word for you."

"What in the world would you need to go to Yale for? Fort Wright has all the programs you would need. It's a proper place for a woman to be educated."

"Yale has a pretty good reputation for education as well," Dallas chuckled. "I think it's good to apply to many schools. See what feels right."

"I agree," Carol slipped in before her mother could protest again. "And Mother, think of all the good men there are at Yale. I'd be lucky to find someone like Dad to marry there." The lie stuck on her tongue and took great effort to dislodge. It wasn't that she didn't think her father was good. As a matter of fact, she found him to be wonderful. But going to Yale, or any other Ivy League school, had nothing to do with finding a husband.

"Well," Francine pursed her lips and considered Carol's argument. "I don't see why we would send you all that way and pay all that money for a degree you won't use."

"Perhaps I will use it," Carol suggested. "You would be surprised how things are changing. I know that's not the case in the circles you are in. Most everyone you associate with feels differently. I can understand that. But for most everyone else in the country, women are starting families and joining the workforce. You know Lance Robins, Lee's son? I was talking to him at a dinner party about a month ago, and he was quite supportive of the idea of a woman with a career."

"Sure," Francine snickered. "Hypothetically. He doesn't

mean he wants to be married to a woman in a business suit who isn't around to cook dinner or keep the house."

Carol nearly did it. She almost reminded her mother that she did neither of those things herself. "Balance would be paramount," Carol offered. "But I think the world is changing and I want to make sure I'm ready to change with it. Maybe I'll take this internship and find I don't care for working in the office or pursuing a role in the publishing industry. Perhaps I'll just get it out of my system."

Those were her mother's words and Carol had been clever enough to weaponize them and get them out first. "I don't know what I'll tell the ladies. All their daughters are either traveling this summer, nannying, or working at the country club for fun," her mother said.

Carol had a response for this as well. "Just tell them that a charming man from Sullivan Books pursued me for the job and I was smitten with the idea. It'll be a fun diversion for the summer, and you and Dad were kind enough to indulge."

The perfectly crafted response left Francine dumbstruck. It was the kind of verbal gymnastics usually performed by the women who'd been competing with each other for decades. A difficult skill that took ages to master. Yet Carol seemed to be fluent suddenly. "We're certainly going to talk more about college," Francine warned. "The plan has always been for you to go to Fort Wright. The nuns there are experts on educating young women."

"I'm only a junior," Carol said, as though an urgent need to design her future wasn't always looming over her head.

"All I'm focused on is trying something new this summer. Like I said, maybe I'll hate it." She, and likely her father, knew damn well she'd fall in love with the job. The pace. The excitement. The immersion into words and art. The bug would bite her and this would not be a phase.

"Fine," Francine acquiesced, taking the letter in her hand and sauntering out of the room. Over her shoulder, she called, "You'd better have time to attend all the events this summer."

"Yes, Mother," Carol said, stifling a squeal. It had worked. She'd navigated all the traps, bitten her tongue when needed, and then made her case.

"Perhaps you should be pursuing law rather than publishing," Dallas whispered. "That was a masterful closing argument you just made." His eyes, pebble gray with specks of blue, flooded with pride. "Sullivan Books is a great opportunity. I could have gotten you in at any of the publishing houses I work with if you'd have asked."

"I wanted to get in on my own merit if possible."

"Anything is possible for you."

"Yale?" she asked, holding her breath as he answered.

"Of course. Nearly all the universities of that caliber are going coed now. If anyone can handle it, I know you can. But your mother is right, it's a lot to invest, both financially and years of your life, if you don't plan to pursue a degree."

A mischievous smile spread across her face. "I would love the chance to follow in your footsteps someday."

"If it's what you really want, you'll surpass me easily.

But I don't know that your mother is ready for all that information right now."

"Baby steps," Carol whispered.

"And you need to continue to meet your social obligations." His face was suddenly serious. "She's not wrong about how important they are for a young woman. The friends you make, the people you surround yourself with via these gatherings will be a crucial part of your life and the opportunities presented to you. At the end of the day, what's most important to me is that you are taken care of after I'm gone."

"Even if it's me taking care of myself?" Carol asked, hope filling her chest.

"I think maybe I'd prefer it." Dallas leaned in and tweaked her nose affectionately. "But if you tell your mother I said that, I'll deny it with my very last breath."

"If she believes you said it, you'll be taking your very last breath."

A genuine wave of joy swept her up. This had been the closest Carol had ever been to the possibility of a future. One she didn't dread. It wouldn't be easy. She'd have to be tactical and precise. But it was practice for the day she'd be running her own company. It wasn't a complete absurdity to consider it. There were women running companies and paving the way. The question was whether or not a woman who was expected, by her peers and family, to live one way, might be able to break that mold. Could she be different than her mother, grandmother and all her great aunts and older cousins?

10

Marta

The liquor store was a relic. Remarkably unchanged over the years. Marta had been coming in with her mother since she was a child. The way some children followed their parent around a hobby store or library. This was more than just an errand on her mother's list. It was a part of the routine. A place to socialize and linger an extra half hour. Play keno or buy a lottery ticket to determine just how many bottles might make it into the shopping cart that day. The memories weren't fond, but they weren't as dark as they sounded either. Marta enjoyed watching the lights on the lottery machine and appreciated the way people swore in front of her. It made her feel a part of something.

Years later, continuing the legacy, she'd bought her first bottle of cheap wine in a jug here even though she wasn't of age. If you claimed it was for your parent, they'd usually let it slide. The walls were still littered with old faded liquor brand advertisements and the shelves were slumping and overfilled. The other thing that hadn't changed was the man behind the counter. Miller was a wiry guy with nervous energy and clothes far too big for his frame. The cuts on his hands were from slinging kegs around and breaking down boxes with a broken knife.

"Hey Miller," Marta said as she pushed open the heavy glass door and the bell overhead jingled.

"Marta?" he asked, clapping three times at the sight of her. "Damn, girl. I thought you were done with this town."

"What can I say, Dreven is just too charming to stay away. I might summer here one day if I can find a little cottage."

"Right," Miller scoffed. "At least if you're going to be here, make sure you have booze."

"A solid plan. I'm going to see Glenn and Sam to talk about my mom. That requires wine." She took one off the shelf and smirked at the cheap spirits she and her friends used to save up to buy. Though she wasn't much of a drinker, there were nights she did allow herself the refuge of a buzz.

"You better card me," she said, pointing her finger accusingly at him. "I don't want to look so old now that you don't need to see my license."

"You look fantastic," Miller announced, checking her out from head to toe. "You just missed Keith by the way."

"Keith?" Her heart stopped and she accidentally banged the bottle of wine hard against the counter. She hadn't lifted it high enough to clear the ledge and it smashed. Glass and red wine exploded all over her outfit and scattered to the floor.

"Holy hell," Miller said, jittering and looking helpless. "What'd you do that for?"

"It was an accident," Marta said, her feet frozen in place as wine dripped down the front of her body. "I'll clean it up. Where is the mop?"

"No," Miller said. "Don't move. I don't want you to cut yourself. Stand right there and I'll clean around you until it's safe."

That was a stupid plan. It made no sense. But Marta felt so terrible that she obliged, standing perfectly still as Miller began frantically sweeping, mopping, and towel drying the floor around her.

"Miller, I am so sorry," she said earnestly as she finally took a step back and he handed over a towel for her clothes. "I don't know what happened."

"You heard me say your ex-husband's name and you smashed a bottle like the Hulk. Damn, I knew you guys got divorced but I thought it was pretty chill."

Marta had wondered if the town had gotten together to place blame for the divorce on one of them. Only a few people knew that Keith had been a miserable husband with a short temper. Even fewer knew he'd been violent. But

Marta had left so abruptly that she assumed after the hate she got in the wake of her father's death, this would be just an extension of that animosity.

"It wasn't that," Marta lied. "I'm jet-lagged from coming back from California. I guess I'm too tired to lift a wine bottle all of a sudden."

"I saw your face when I said Keith's name. Do I see a love bird reunion in your future?" Miller grinned his jovial smile, but apparently her reaction sent it wobbling off his face.

"Uh, no reunion." She tried to keep her voice steady. "I'm actually trying to avoid almost everyone on this trip. But I forgot just how connected everyone is in a small town."

"At least you aren't drawing attention to yourself then," Miller teased as he gestured to the trash can full of wine-stained glass.

"Ring me up for the broken one and the replacement," Marta said, grabbing another bottle.

"No way," Miller shot back. "The store will cover it. It was an accident. I'm just happy to see you back around here."

She almost said it was good to be back. But it wasn't. "I'm sorry again for the mess. Glenn will get a kick out of seeing me covered in wine." Marta was stalling, teetering on the idea of asking how long ago Keith left. If he was still driving that green two-door pickup truck. The fear that Miller would misread her questions was worrisome. The last thing she needed was a rumor going around that she was in town to see Keith.

"Thanks Miller, you're always looking out for everyone around here."

"Well, if I'm going to sell this poison to everyone the least I can do is offer it with a smile and some kind words. I always make sure to chat with your mom every time she's in."

"And how often is that these days?" Marta asked, afraid to hear the answer.

"Two or three times a week now. I worry about her." Miller's fluttering eyes and jittering hands made him look as if he could barely keep his thoughts straight, let alone have time to care about everyone who walked into the liquor store. Yet Marta always knew him to be sweet and empathetic. The world she was finally being invited into, the one that existed in San Diego or anywhere else her career might take her, wouldn't have room for Miller. He'd be written off as a tweaker or a failure. No one would look closely enough or listen intently enough to see just how loyal and friendly Miller was. It made her heart tighten up and her mind swirl. For everything she might gain, it was impossible to overlook the things she'd have to leave behind.

"I really appreciate you being so kind to her. I have a hard time with that. I wish I knew how to help, or if she even wanted help." Marta fidgeted with her keys and thought of what her mother was probably doing right now. Something self-destructive or unhealthy.

"I get it," Miller replied somberly. "People who need the

most love can be so unlovable. Maybe one of these days she'll surprise you."

Marta smiled and hugged the wine bottle closer. "You're a good man, Miller. You're what I love about this town. It's a short list, but you're on it."

"I'll die here," Miller said unemotionally. All his twitching and ticks seemed to stop for a moment. "And I'm okay with that. But I'll be mad if you do. Make sure you're only passing through."

"Just long enough to fix my family and my reputation," she joked as he handed her the change.

"Don't even kid about that," he said, narrowing his eyes. "Try something with better odds like getting struck by lightning or climbing Everest."

With a laugh and wave, Marta made her way back to her car. The dread was already coursing through her veins. There would be a time when she'd likely have to face Keith again, but the liquor store parking lot this late at night was not ideal. Luckily, there was no sign of him. Instead, she spotted a few girls who'd graduated a year or two ahead of her. Turning her head and moving quickly to her car, she dodged them. It was turning into a mental video game. She was keeping score of how many familiar faces she could avoid.

The neon lights of the liquor store faded in her rearview mirror as she headed over to Glenn's house. She wouldn't tell him about meeting up with Eddy today or their conversation. He wouldn't understand. Hell, she was still trying to understand it all. Instead, they'd fill their conversation with quips about their mother's dysfunction and maybe try to plan some solutions. Glenn would be pleased to know Terrance was coming back tomorrow. Another ally in the fight. Or another casualty of the war. She wasn't quite sure yet.

11

Carol

Robert was due in her office any minute. And like a young woman waiting for her date to knock on her door, Carol could feel the nerves. She quickly chastised herself for the silly response. Robert, an important member of the board, was not someone she should be starting a relationship with. Even the fluttering of her heart, the wandering of her mind, was dangerous. A distraction she couldn't afford. There was too much on the line.

Terrance had left for the airport which meant Robert's arrival could go fairly unnoticed. But there was another problem created by that. No gatekeeper to her office. No one to keep out the people she didn't want to see.

"Carol," Eli boomed as he stepped into her office, knocking and walking straight in.

"Eli," she snipped. "That's not how knocking works. You're supposed to wait for me to tell you to come in."

He rolled his eyes. "You're not in here having a pillow fight in your panties, right?"

"If you say the word panties again, I'm calling security." Carol wasn't afraid of Eli. Logic told her she should be leery of his motivations and the possible consequences of his retribution. But for some reason, he just seemed like such a small man. Something she could swat away like a fly. It was likely an underestimation, but she hated to even consider him a threat.

"Oh, right," Eli sat down in the chair in front of her desk and offered a funny look. "We can't even be in this office alone, right? That's how things are now. It would be my word against yours if anything happened and men like me are never believed."

Carol's blood boiled. "Maybe men like you have an integrity problem. If you have a problem being believed, there must be a reason."

"Oh, there's a reason. About half the population is the reason. Your half," he huffed. "But we're not going to solve that mess today. That's not why I'm here."

"Here to collect the rat you mailed to my office?" Carol leaned back in her chair and watched closely for a reaction. He offered none. Not a twitch of the lip or a flicker of his eyes.

"Rat?" he asked, sounding surprised. "What rat?"

"Okay," she laughed as if he weren't worth her time. "What are you here for?"

"A meeting." He raised his brow and his hair plugs danced comically. "I want to discuss this business about the award recipient."

"I have a calendar I keep up to date. I have an assistant who could schedule it for you. Feel free to reach out to Terrance and find some time I have open."

"Terrance," Eli scoffed. Carol felt every hair on the back of her neck stand up. She had no problem putting up with Eli's attacks, but she would not allow him to target Terrance.

"I wouldn't say his name that way," Carol warned. "He's a better man than you in about every measure there is."

"He likes working for a woman who likes to keep her heel on his neck?" Eli narrowed his eyes. "Don't you think it's strange he doesn't mind taking orders from you?"

"I think it's strange that you believe my job requires me to give orders. Maybe that's why you aren't in charge here anymore. One of the many reasons, I would assume."

Eli's face tightened and his color flushed. "I'm not here because putting you in the job pacified some bleeding-heart equality freaks. And now you're not even bright enough to realize I'm here to help you. I already know your girl hasn't signed the contract yet. That's a good thing."

"We're not sitting here exchanging insults. I understand you have nothing but time, however, I'm running a company. The decisions I make are not your concern."

"I will speak plainly. Under no circumstances will this girl and her background taint the long history of this establishment."

"Eli, you have no power here. I'm sorry for how that must feel for you." Carol's voice was flat and unapologetic.

"I have power everywhere," Eli said smugly. "I am sure you know that about me by now."

"I know that you use coercion and blackmail to keep people under your thumb. That doesn't worry me. I don't cower to threats and I don't leave myself open to slander and extortion. You can dig as deep as you want into my life. Have at it."

"I know that you're lily-white and prudish." Eli sneered. "I wouldn't waste my time looking for something interesting or scandalous with you. And I don't have to. I've had something compelling enough to sway you for the last thirty years. I never thought you'd rise high enough in the ranks or become important enough for me to use it."

Carol thought back over the last thirty years of her life and didn't bat an eye at his threat. Growing up, as this path became clear, integrity was paramount. Her father had instilled the need for an unwavering ability to be trusted and worthy of the position she was always trying to attain. Eli was a fool to play this card with her. "Eli you're grasping at straws. You aren't going to impugn my reputation. I'm not worried."

"I'm not talking about you. But what I do know is there is one person who means more to you than even your own standing in this industry. The legacy of your father is pretty grand. Certainly one of the greats."

Just as she felt a snap of defensiveness at the mention of Terrance, Carol boiled with rage. "You don't get to talk about my father or his legacy. You are the exact kind of man he worked to get rid of."

"I love how children think they know their parents. As if they could ever understand them as real people. Flawed and damaged. Your father and I crossed paths. We knew many of the same people. Ran in the same circles. I can assure you, it would be easy for me to shine light on who he really was."

Now Carol was the one to scoff. "My father was a beloved member of this industry for most of his life. People know you're a weasel. Your credibility is so damaged. No one will take rumors you spread seriously."

"I agree," Eli replied smugly. "But it wouldn't be just some hearsay. I can assure you, it would be enough to ruin him."

Carol slammed her hand on her desk and stood up, sending her chair into the wall behind her. "Get out." She pointed at her office door. "Just when I think you can't sink any lower, you take aim at my dead father's legacy."

"It's him who ruined it. I'd just finally be exposing him." Eli leaned back in his chair and propped his arms up behind his head casually.

"You fu—"

"Hey," Robert said, bursting into her office. "What the hell is going on here?" His face was painted with concern and then scorn as he settled on Eli lounging in the chair across from Carol.

"Robert?" Eli stammered, sitting up and looking startled. "Carol and I were just—"

"Save it," Robert replied, cutting his hand through the air. "I can guess exactly what you're doing in here, and it's done now. You're leaving."

Eli laughed. "I liked it much better when you were a team player, Robert." Even with the blustery reply, he was standing and obediently moving toward the door.

"We're not on the same team," Robert reminded him. "I have an actual meeting to discuss board business with Carol. Whatever you're doing is just noise."

"You two have business?" Eli looked at the folder in Robert's hands and looked desperate to investigate it.

"Yes, Carol actually cares about how her employees feel. We're reviewing the employee engagement survey and creating an action plan for the coming year. I doubt you ever even reviewed the results."

Eli narrowed his eyes and appraised Robert closely. "Don't fall under her spell, man." He gestured to Carol. "You're better than this."

Robert took two steps closer to Eli. "You're in this woman's office doing whatever it takes to try to advance your archaic agenda. Slimy tactics and throwing your weight around. All in the name of being a 'man's man.' Those days are over Eli, and so is this meeting." With a few subtle movements of his body, Robert was edging Eli out of the room and shutting the door.

"Pig," Carol cursed under her breath as she tried to regain her composure. She normally prided herself on not allowing men like Eli to get a rise out of her. But here she was, standing and looking ready for a fistfight.

"Are you all right?" Robert asked, his voice layered with concern. "What was he saying?"

"Oh, you know, just dragging my father's name through the mud and threatening to do so publicly if I didn't give in to his demands. My father was an amazing man. He was principled and reliable. Fair and trustworthy. For Eli to come in here and tell me that he would expose some other version of my father is just asinine."

"He's getting desperate." Robert rounded the desk and put his hand gently on her shoulder. "I am sure your father was a great man."

"Damn right. And he worked hard to make progress in this industry and the world. When there was no path forward for me to work and advance my career, he helped me forge one. If he were alive today, he'd be championing Marta just like I am. This place needs her."

"Why?" Robert asked, not accusingly but with genuine intrigue.

"Why?" Carol parroted back, turning toward him, pleased to have him so close by again. "This award, this whole industry, has been filled with elite people whose trajectory is already sky-high. They don't need this award to advance their already privileged lives. Some perfect pedigree and Ivy League diploma is the key that has always opened the doors to this building."

"But Marta would be different?"

"She is different," Carol explained, her voice high and urgent. "All these people, the ones we shower with accolades, wrote their books at their family's vineyard or while staring out over the peaks of a ski mountain from the warmth of the lodge. Can they craft beautiful works? Of course. But all from the same perspective. Every year we run this piece, showing where they are from and what they've done. Who are we inspiring? What are we trying to prove?"

"I suppose it's to highlight the traditional path?"

"Marta wrote her flawless and magnificent book between serving customers in a dusty bookstore and waiting tables at a small restaurant. She developed characters from her own trauma, born out of her own desire to understand it. Her book is therapy. It's art rooted in life, not some performative piece trying to emulate it. There is an authenticity to what she created and just because that doesn't come with an Ivy League education and from a certain zip code doesn't mean we should overlook it. The fact that we exclude people based on who they are or where they are from is an abomination. I have worked for decades, putting so much of my own life on hold, so that I could rise to this exact position and enact some changes. I finally get here and there is still a man trying to stand in my way. Still holding on with a death grip to the way things always have been. Marta is not a charity case. She does not diminish the status of our establishment. She adds to it. She's texture and depth we've never been brave enough to explore. Let the cowards move aside. I'm not stopping until we can look back and have something to be proud of. Someone who can be proud they joined us."

"Why haven't you said that?" Robert had dropped his hand from her shoulder but stood intimately close as he dipped his head to look her in the eyes.

"Said what?"

"All of that. In the boardroom, you showed us metrics and talked about viewer engagement and changing demographics. Why didn't you say all of that? I supported Marta because I believed in you. Now, after all that, I believe in her."

A rush of adrenaline coursed through Carol as she considered his question. "Are you crazy?" she asked, her eyes wide with disbelief. "Do you think I'm granted the luxury of a rant? I'd be labeled hysterical. Emotional. Hormonal. I don't get to lose my cool or give some impassioned speech if it makes people too uncomfortable. I have to sell my ideas. Quietly persuade. All while being both demure and resilient."

"I found it to be an impassioned plea." Robert looked empathetic. "If you feel this strongly about Marta and those are your reasons, people need to know. Eli isn't going to sit around and quietly explain why he disagrees. Sometimes you've got to meet fire with fire."

"You know what they do to women with fire? They burn us as witches."

Robert chuckled and she broke into a smile. For all the

pressure and the risk, there was still something sweet about this.

"I thought you were supposed to be bringing lunch during these meetings?" Her eyes fluttered and she eyed the measly folders in his hands.

"I stashed it at Terrance's desk when I heard Eli in here." Robert looked like a teenage boy who'd just skillfully climbed through his girlfriend's window, undetected by her parents.

"You did?" A giddy laugh escaped her as he stepped out of her office, peered around for any witnesses and then snuck back with a brown bag in his hand.

"Tell me that's gyros."

"I'm a man of my word." He placed the bag down in front of her and did a small playful bow. "I know gyros won't make everything better."

"They'll help," she said, gesturing for him to close the door while she unwrapped the food. "I can at least enjoy this, and the good company, while I plot my next move."

"I love plotting moves," Robert replied excitedly. "How can I help?"

"I need Marta to sign the contract." Carol felt her chest tighten with anxiety. If that part didn't happen, if Marta bailed, Carol would look like a fool. Her judgment would be called into question and doubt would surely be cast upon her in her role.

"It sounds like you sent the best man for the job to convince Marta. Terrance will work all his charming magic to convince her to sign the contract. If he flashes a few of those smiles and maybe throws in a wink, she'll be clamoring for a pen."

Carol hummed out a laugh. "Terrance has a lot of tools in his toolbox. I have no doubt if there is a way for this to work, he'll find it. It won't be easy, but it'll be worth it." Her mind wandered to her father. The way he'd worked so hard to change the industry for her. For women of the future. The arrows Eli shot at her should have bounced right off the armor around her heart. She knew her father and the kind of man he was. There would be nothing Eli could say that would tarnish his legacy. And yet she felt pierced; some of those nasty arrows had made it through.

"But that's not what's worrying you," Robert said incisively. "Eli really bothered you today."

"I was never worried about what he might do or say about me." Carol finally took a seat in her chair and looked at the ceiling.

"But you want to protect your father's memory."

"I wouldn't be here if it weren't for my father's hard work and the path he blazed. Not a lot of people in this industry can say the same. He was a pioneer, always focusing on making the circle wider, bringing all different types of people in."

"His reputation is impressive," Robert agreed. "And I'm not saying Eli is telling the truth or his threat has any merit at all, but sometimes we don't know everything about people. Even the people we love. It's hard when we find out our parents are fallible beings. It's important for you to know even if there is something you find out about your father, it doesn't tarnish all the things he did for you and others. People are not all good or all bad."

She nodded but the comfort wasn't enough to fully wrap around her. "I might need something more than just a gyro," she whispered, picking it up and taking a bite.

Reaching into his pocket, Robert pulled out a bag of gummy worms. "These were supposed to be for my ride home, but you need them more."

"You're spoiling me."

"With the eight-dollar gyros and two-dollar gummy worms?"

"With any kind of treat," Carol explained. "When you're a capable woman who takes care of herself, people don't think you need little surprises or a little something to get through the day."

"Everyone deserves someone looking out for them."

"That used to be my father," Carol sighed. "When I lost him, I lost my biggest advocate and protector. Life was never the same. It was just me and my mother then. That was hell."

"Mothers and daughters can struggle. My ex and my daughter had some rough years too. I'm sure becoming a widow didn't help your mom."

"This wasn't normal mother-daughter drama. It's hard to explain just how bad it was. But I recently cleaned out the attic at my childhood home. My mother's journals were there."

"Don't read them," Robert offered quickly.

"That's what my friend said too. I just wish I understood

what made my mother so angry. Why she seemed to hate me so much."

"I'm sure she didn't write the answers in there. Self-reflection is not something people come by easily, and they certainly don't do it when they are writing in their personal journals. That's where they tell themselves what they want to hear. Tell themselves how right they are. Don't get me wrong, it's healthy. I just think if she wanted you to read them, she'd have been more deliberate about it."

"Or," Carol said with a teasing grin, "and hear me out. Maybe she left them up there because she wanted to make sure I read them."

"Maybe," Robert agreed. "But did she do a lot of things that you found to be intentionally hurtful?"

"Almost everything."

"Then maybe leaving the journals where you can find them is just one more way to try to wound you. I say leave them be."

Carol nodded and painted on a sweet, agreeable smile. Inside she already knew it was too late. Her mind was made up now that she heard Eli threatening her father's legacy. Maybe there would be something in those journals that could tip her off. She knew robbing Eli of the element of surprise was key. There couldn't possibly be anything else her mother could do or say that would damage her even more. Though even from the grave, her mother likely was capable of it.

12

Carol – Age Twenty-three

"You haven't cured cancer." Francine batted her lashes dramatically at her daughter who stood in her cap and gown. "You would think with all this pomp and circumstance they'd expect that you'd done something exceptional."

"Well," Carol asserted, "some might say graduating with honors would be something exceptional." She ignored her mother's humming noise and instead straightened her cap, smiling at herself in the mirror.

"And now what?" Francine asked antagonistically.

"The ceremony starts at nine." Carol answered this way to be obstinate. She knew her mother was well aware of the time they needed to leave. This question was cutting and she'd have to stay on her guard.

"I mean where are you going to hang the degree once they give it to you today? You have no house. No prospects for a husband anymore. Breaking things off with Myron was your downfall. It'll be that thing you look back on and regret deeply."

"I wish you didn't say those things with such a smile, Mother." Carol's chest burned with frustration. It didn't matter how many times she rehearsed her arguments or anticipated her mother's impending scorn, she was wholly unprotected.

"Trust me," Francine said, turning her lips down sharply. "Nothing about this situation makes me happy. You've spent years of your life getting an education for a career that doesn't exist. These were prime years you could have been socializing and raising your status in our circles. It's lost time."

"I loved college," Carol asserted. "It wasn't lost time for me. And wherever I hang my diploma, I'll be proud of it."

Her father cleared his throat as he entered the room. A kind of warning alarm that if they were arguing, he wouldn't want to hear it. "You'll hang your diploma in your office."

"I don't have one of those," Carol said somberly. For as determined as she was to prove her mother wrong, she was sad that she hadn't lived up to the dreams her father allowed her to keep.

"Sure you do." He beamed in that silly way he always did when he was holding on to a secret.

"I have a chair in the corner of the lobby at Sullivan

Books. I don't think they want me hanging anything out there."

"You advanced from an unpaid summer intern to assistant to the junior editor."

"Not at lightning speed," she reminded him.

"Sullivan doesn't know how much of an asset you are. They'll realize it when you put your notice in next week."

"My notice?" Carol asked, tensing with fear. Maybe her father had grown tired of her silly aspirations too. Perhaps he'd join forces with her mother. There would be no fighting it if they unified.

"You'll be starting with Quincy Parker Publishing and Arts at the end of the month. They've brought you on as an editor. No junior for you. There is an enormous amount of room for advancement in different facets of the arts. The opportunities for you to succeed there would be endless. Music, movies, all forms of the arts would become open to you."

Carol swelled with joy and then deflated suddenly. "You arranged this?"

"Of course, I did," he replied curtly. "That doesn't mean you don't deserve it."

"I told you I'd like to be hired somewhere on my own merits. Sullivan Books might not have many opportunities, but at least I know I'm there because of my own hard work."

"You should be well beyond assistant to a junior editor at this point. I know you'd like to advance based on your own merits, but all they see is a woman when you walk in their building. They don't see how much talent you have. They keep putting up barriers and it's not right. This isn't me throwing my weight around in the industry so that you can be favored. I just want you to have a fair shot. The same you would have if you were my son."

"Why do you do this?" Francine bellowed dramatically. "At some point, she'll realize there is no place for her and she'll settle into the life where she belongs. But if you keep pulling strings, you'll just prolong the inevitable."

"Things are changing, Mother," Carol argued. "There is legislation in the works today that could allow women to get their own credit cards, build their own wealth. Look at Katherine Graham. She's the CEO of the company that owns the Washington Post. She's one of the most powerful people in publishing. There are anti-discrimination laws to make sure I'm able to work the same positions as a man. Gloria Steinem just spoke at the national press club. Now is exactly the time to find my place in this industry. Women, strong women, are paving my way."

Francine stomped her foot. "Katherine Graham's husband killed himself. Steinem is just stirring the pot and causing more division. If these women are your heroes, there will never be a man interested in you."

"Oh no," Carol said, pretending to feel faint, placing the back of her hand on her forehead. "A man won't want me if I'm successful?"

"A man won't want you if you're a work-obsessed woman who is just trying to outdo him. A woman who can't care for her home and entertain his company."

"I don't want a man who won't celebrate my success. I understand there was a time not very long ago that getting a man to love you and marry you was a matter of survival. It wasn't an option to go out and start a career that could actually sustain you. His income was the woman's income as well, and so being amicable and dependent was self-preservation. Those days are coming to an end. When I am in a relationship, it will be because I'm seen for who I am not for what I need."

"The world has not changed that much," Francine said, her finger waggling fiercely in Carol's direction. "Even if you do manage to make yourself enough money to survive, your life will be empty. A woman is not whole until she has a family."

Carol gasped at the words that flew in the face of everything she believed. Everything strong women were out marching to disprove. "I'm truly filled with sadness for you," Carol uttered slowly. "If you believe there is only one way to live, one way to be whole, you're missing so much of life. I refuse to believe the path you took is the only one." She chuckled sarcastically. "I don't even believe it's made you happy. You just want to shove other people down the same route. Maybe to make yourself feel better."

Carol expected her mother to bark back something cutting. Instead, it was her father who spoke up. "Do not speak to your mother that way." His voice was stern. "She may not agree with your choices but she deserves your respect."

Silence fell between them all until Carol processed his assertion. “You’re right. I’m sorry, Mother.”

Pursed lips and an upturned nose was all Francine would offer back. She glided out of the room without another word.

“She means well,” Dallas whispered, putting a hand on Carol’s shoulder. “You need to follow your own path, but know it’s going to hurt her to watch.”

“Why can’t she be happy for me?” Carol asked, a tear rolling down her cheek. “It shouldn’t hurt her to see me find joy and purpose.”

“When we have children, we plan their entire lives in our minds. We rock you and feed you and it’s quite boring.” He chuckled and wiped her tear. “So while we sit there and watch you fuss or learn some new little skill, we imagine the life you’ll have. Your mother was very invested in the one she designed for you. It was more than just a figment of her imagination. She put real work into it. Time and energy.”

“Do you think she’d actually be proud of me if I did things her way? She’d be planning a wedding by now. I’d be in dress shops talking about delicate lace patterns. Picking out cocktail napkins and centerpieces. Would things be different?”

“No,” Dallas edged out reluctantly. “She’d still find something to be upset about.”

“Why?” The complexities of her mother’s personality seemed endless. The most hardened explorers would not be able to map its depth.

"That's just in her nature. That's one reason I want you to follow your passion. I don't want that penchant for displeasure and dissatisfaction to be our family legacy. There is a role your mother must play. Many women before her have had to do the same. It's a mix of martyr and mastermind. This kind of selfless yet strategic balance. I don't want that for you. Take the job being offered. It's a chance to break the cycle."

"It doesn't feel right to get a job based only on your endorsement of me." Carol had mixed feelings about the opportunity. It would seem like a blemish to start at a new company where everyone knew she'd gotten hired because of her father. On the other hand, she'd be unlikely to ever get the chance without him.

"I'm not doing it for you," he replied, desperation in his voice. "You have to be the first so there is room someday for the second and third. You have to rise as high as you can and as you climb, lift others up. People who might never have the chance otherwise. Yes, my reputation in this industry will open doors for you. But they mustn't be squandered opportunities. When it's your hand on the doorknob, swing it open for someone else."

It felt improbable to even imagine that someday she'd be in a position to create change. To form it and force it at her will. But his words created an energy inside of her. Enough of a shock to swing her from apprehension to excitement.

"Do you really think that's possible?" she asked, a flurry

of visions of the future flipping through her mind. Power suits and conference calls.

"It has to be." A crushing look of regret washed over his face. "I need you to do this for our family. So that you can be better than what came before.

"You're too good to me, Dad," Carol said, hugging him tightly. "You're the best man in the whole world."

"Don't say that," Dallas replied, an edge to his voice.

"Why?" She giggled but he didn't soften.

"Because I've made mistakes. Lots of them. When I hear you say how great I am, it makes me feel like a fraud." He turned his face away as she released him from the hug.

Looking back on all the years she'd been observing him, no imperfection could be found. A couple of shaky business deals that all ended up working out. Maybe he meant his marriage to her mother. Carol could understand how regret might have seeped in. But surely none of it was his fault. Not enough to have his features twisting like this.

"What do you mean?" she pressed. Not usually one to pry, her words took him by surprise.

"Oh, it's not important. I just want to make things right. Make the world more welcoming to everyone. Your career is the perfect place to start. If you want that, I want it for you too."

"I do," Carol said through a bright smile, hoping it was contagious. Whether forced or not, he met her grin with his own.

"I used to say things like *your mother will come around. She'll understand someday*. I'm not sure that's true, and you're too old to lie to. I think you'll need to do what you like in spite of how she feels. Just don't ever do things *because* of how she feels. Be stronger than that."

The advice felt layered with a million unsaid things. Words she couldn't guess and twisted meanings she couldn't unravel. Instead she just nodded, kissed his cheek and watched him leave the room.

Graduation, that triumphant crossing of the stage, was the accomplishment she imagined. Her parents played their roles, never straying from the characters and script they always followed. In front of others, her mother was doting and bubbly. Her father chattered about the future and his pride. They clapped when her name was called but it was the family of another student she envied. The ruckus group that hooted and hollered when their son crossed the stage. They stood and made a scene. It wasn't about what other people thought. For them, it was about making sure the person who mattered knew he was loved. Out loud.

As the ceremony ended, Carol daydreamed about her future. The job that was now waiting for her. A head start she never thought she'd have. Where some might feel immense pressure, she felt motivation. Whatever weighed down her father, her success would be the thing to lift it off of him. And nothing would stop her.

13

Marta

Denying it would be lying to herself. The anticipation was intense. Terrance had flown over last minute to support her. To comfort her. To fortify her belief in herself. Though they'd shared an intense kiss, that wasn't the most impactful thing that had passed between them. It had been his encouragement. The permission to believe in the impossible. That had her craving his return. Well, that and his gorgeous eyes and captivating smile.

"Miss me?" he asked playfully as he threw his suitcase in the trunk of her small car and hopped in the front seat.

She nearly blurted out just how much she'd missed him. But instead, she gave him a playful and annoyed glare. "I told you that you didn't have to come so quick. You can't drop everything just because I sound like I'm falling apart."

"I didn't drop everything." He shook his head. "This is exactly where I'm supposed to be."

"What hotel did you book? There are a few in the city. I can point you in the direction of the one least likely to get you robbed."

"I didn't book a hotel," he explained coolly. "I'll grab a room wherever you are."

"There are better ones," she cut back quickly. "Somewhere you'll be more comfortable."

"Close to you is comfortable." He gave her that half-smile that sent a tingle up her spine. "Plus we're going to be out and about anyway. It doesn't matter where I sleep."

Marta fought the urge to imagine where he'd sleep and offer him a spot near her. In the few days they'd been away from each other, she'd convinced herself the heat she felt growing between them wasn't so hot. Circumstances and adrenaline fueled the intensity. But now that he was back by her side, she had to face the facts. It required willpower to keep her hands off his body and her mind off her feelings for him.

"We should go back and see your mother together," he offered, trying to sound upbeat.

He'd accidentally found the antidote for whatever love potion she'd apparently swigged. Nothing zapped the romance and visions of a secret tryst like talk of visiting her mother.

"I wouldn't do that to you," she chuckled. "I like you too much."

"It's what I'm here for, no matter how much you like me."

"You'll never look at me the same once you actually start to take a peek at what my life is really like."

"Your mother is not your life. She's a person biologically related to you. And frankly at this point, from my perspective, she's a barrier to your success. That puts her and me on opposing sides."

The visual was reassuring. It felt nice to be lined up, ready for battle. Especially as she felt her side growing. Last night she'd laughed with her brother Glenn and sister-in-law, Sammy. They were on her side. Terrance and Carol were standing by her. Even if they lived a few hours away in the town she ran to, Heather and Ray had her back too. It wasn't enough, but it was a start. It was more than she'd had last week.

"Invite her to lunch today," Terrance suggested. "I'm not trying to minimize all the baggage or pretend we can fix it over one meal. But maybe some neutral territory and someone she's just met could be enough to at least get through a normal conversation.

"Normal conversation is a very high bar." Marta pulled the car into the parking garage of the hotel and drew in a deep breath. "I'll ask her to come out. But she'll only eat at a few places. Creature of habit. Or maybe it's more that she won't try new things."

"I'm not picky," Terrance said, turning in the passenger

seat to face her. "But I do need a hot shower and breakfast. Want to join me?"

"Careful," Marta warned, raising a brow at him. "It sounds like you're inviting me into the shower."

"That would be highly inappropriate," Terrance replied, pretending to clutch some imaginary pearls. "Just breakfast. And we should probably have our clothes on for that."

"To keep it professional?"

"Exactly." Terrance checked his phone and read something briefly, then grimaced.

Marta felt instantly guilty. "You should be in California helping Carol. You're a big part of her life. I'm sure you keep everything moving smoothly."

"I don't like leaving her," Terrance admitted. "It's not like she's incapable. The woman can move mountains. I just like to clear the path when I can. I don't like that Eli's targeting her. I want to wring that guy's neck. He's everything that's wrong with men today."

"It's like an endless game of whack-a-mole. Even if you hit that jerk with the hammer, other nasty guys pop back up."

"We just need more hammers."

They chatted lightheartedly and she basked in his presence. She was so happy he came back. Terrance gestured to the elevator as they made their way through the parking garage. Marta was suddenly self-conscious of the hotel she'd picked. While it was nicer than she'd usually have sprung for, she was certain it wouldn't live up to Terrance's usual vacation spots. It looked out over the river, but the river had seen better days.

"This place is nothing special," Marta said, shrugging off the lobby as they entered. "There are other hotels if you go a little farther down the highway.

"This entire trip, please don't apologize for your hometown or who you're related to. I don't scare easy. Growing up with my aunt and uncle, we had enough to get by, but I don't come from some swanky upscale place myself."

"I don't know if everyone will be quite as forgiving as you. Dreven is the town everyone will associate with me. The place that made me, and trust me, this assembly line doesn't have a lot of quality control. They aren't turning out stellar products."

He chuckled and she felt a warm glow in her chest. "You'll have to put that in your next book."

"If there is one," Marta corrected.

"You'll write dozens of books if that's what you want. The difference will be that before you write a word, you'll be paid six figures."

"Six figures," she scoffed. "No one is going to pay me that much."

Terrance stopped and touched her arm gently, turning her toward him. "Marta, that's what's in your future when you sign that contract. There will be a press release and then your phone will start ringing. Well, your agent's phone."

"I don't have one of those," she reminded him.

"You'll need one. Someone reputable." Terrance had a serious look suddenly. "I can't really connect you with anyone. It might be a conflict of interest. But I can point you in the right direction."

"I'm going to be in over my head," Marta said through her tightly set jaw. It was more than just whether or not the world would accept her and the baggage she carried. There was all the change and expectation that would follow if it did work out.

"One step at a time," Terrance replied gently. "Shower. Breakfast. Sight-seeing. Then lunch with your mom. Let's get through that first."

"You're going to have to figure out how you're going to get through the roast beef sandwich at the Cow Barn Tavern. I hope you packed antacids."

He grimaced. "Make sure you're never in charge of writing the travel brochure for this place. No one would ever come visit. I think you're selling it short. When the producers and camera crews come, they'll find the charm. It's here."

"If they find that, they deserve a raise," Marta teased.

"Movie magic," Terrance promised. "Tell me what your favorite place here used to be."

"The highway sign that showed I was leaving." Marta sat in a plush chair in the lobby and eyed the large ice-packed pitcher of fruit-infused water. She had the urge to fill multiple cups and chug it down. The allure of something free and fancy sometimes had her wanting to cast her attempts at looking normal aside. Now with Terrance as her audience, she'd have another reason to behave.

"There must be something. A park. A movie theater. A

place. Somewhere you used to love to hang out with your friends." Terrance handed over his credit card to the woman checking him in but didn't take his eyes off Marta for long. She wanted to give him something. Some picturesque corner of this town that made her feel all warm and fuzzy. Some place that would play well for the cameras when they eventually came to follow her around. It actually pained her to be stumped.

The woman behind the desk chimed in as she handed over his room key. "There is a beautiful river walk with some lovely restaurants just down Millville Lane. Or if you'd like to check out one of the museums—"

Marta interrupted. "He's talking about Dreven, not here." They weren't far from the Dreven line but this was distant enough that the crime and social decay could be intentionally overlooked. Here there was a bit of culture. Some decent places to eat. Even some nice historical sites. It's why she'd chosen to drive the extra miles and pretend.

"Oh," the woman replied sheepishly. "I don't know Dreven well."

"You're lucky." Marta stood and leaned over to see what floor Terrance would be on.

"Don't worry, we're neighbors." He chuckled. "I made sure of it."

"Go take your shower," she insisted, waving for him to head upstairs. "I'm going to stay down here and call my mom. I'll try to think of somewhere decent to take you in Dreven. Or"—she raised a finger up in the air thoughtfully —"we could just stay around here. Actually enjoy ourselves for the day. This town is much better than Dreven."

"I came to see Dreven," Terrance replied flatly. "It can't be that bad."

She cupped her hand to her ear pretending to hear something far off. "Did you hear that? The whole town of Dreven just got together and said, *challenge accepted.*"

14

Marta – Nineteen Years Old

It was a shame she'd done too good of a job. All the energy she'd put into making sure Keith was perceived by all their friends and family as a good man had been too convincing. She'd built him up so high that no one would believe he deserved the fall that would come from the truth. She'd protected his reputation. Covered for his flaws. Defended his outbursts so convincingly people found a way to overlook the madness.

The old skill she'd honed of sensing danger had worked for a while. She could try, with all her might, to make sure there would be nothing to set him off. But eventually, even that failed. Keith was a wildly unhappy man. His parents were loud, obnoxious, and weaponized the idea of withholding love. It was actually what had drawn her to him at first.

Keith was starved for love. It wasn't as if he was walking around begging for attention or pandering to women. Quite the opposite. He was indifferent to a relationship. Most times he was publicly cold and aloof. But then, like a secret passage only she knew the way to open, he'd let her in. She'd be the one he'd share his pain with. No one else understood. This rough, unpleasant man was actually hurting, and she was the balm that could heal his wounds.

The vulnerability, which now she wasn't sure was genuine at all, had been the allure. It seemed the perfect balance. To the world, he was aggressive and protective. Two things she thought she needed. He could block the bad—all the pain—that might come her way. Tough enough to take it and allow her to hide safely behind him. Then in private, he could lean on her. She could listen and comfort.

Things did not, however, fall so neatly in place. Some things worked for a while. Keith was adept at making her feel abundantly safe in public. He knew things. Understood people. Seemed to be able to spot a bad situation or an untrustworthy person without hesitation. He could win a fistfight. Drive confidently through the most complicated high traffic situations without batting an eye. Nerves of steel. Marta had spent so much of her life with her head on a swivel, hyper-vigilant and on edge. Suddenly Keith was there to do all the thinking. To be ready in any situation. The beginning of their relationship felt liberating. She could finally let her guard down and know she was safe.

But that transfer of power had left her weak. He made all the decisions because they'd agreed he was better at it. More equipped. More street smart and worldly. Soon Keith began shifting how he spoke to her. She'd allowed herself to be the dumb one in the relationship. The one in need. And he'd begun reinforcing narrative that every chance he had. Verbally reminding her he was in charge, that she didn't understand how things worked or how people were. Marta had bowed down to him at the start, but he kept his foot on her back to ensure she stayed there. There was no growth. No evolution.

"Girls' nights are an excuse to mess around on your husband," Keith barked, waving his beer as though he were giving a speech.

"It's not," Marta said, huffing with annoyance. "It's not even girls' night. It's the middle of the afternoon. Linda has been on me for months to go out and catch up."

"Linda is disgusting." He twisted his face up as though he'd just smelled something terrible. "All my buddies have stories about her. What do you think it looks like when my wife goes out with someone like that?"

"Your friends talk like that about everyone. Linda is not like that. And we're going out for lunch and shopping. You're making a big deal out of nothing."

"Why can't she just come hang out here? Have you ever asked yourself that? Our house isn't good enough. That should tell you something about her."

She bit her tongue and didn't bother answering with the truth. Keith wouldn't accept that he was the reason none of her friends would come around. “I’m going to lunch with Linda,” Marta said, just as she’d practiced. This was the line in the sand she’d promised herself she would draw. There was no turning back now.

“Don’t do that,” he chuckled. “Don’t try to be a tough guy with me. If you’d actually listened to what I was saying, you’d agree with me.”

“You go out with your friends,” she shot back.

“You and I are very different people,” he answered smugly. “I pay attention to things. I know what’s going on around me and how to deal with people. When I’m not around, you don’t have a clue. I wish you’d listen to me.”

“And I wish I could actually go see my friends.”

“Don’t put that on me. Don’t act like I’m the guy who tells you what you can and can’t do.” He scoffed. “You know damn well how much I have helped you over the years. Look at what you have now because of me. And I barely ask anything of you. Just respect. Respect the fact that I don’t want you going out with someone who has the kind of disgusting reputation Linda does. It reflects bad on both of us. But that’s too much, right? I’m asking too much.”

Marta gulped, pulled her purse over her shoulder, and headed for the door. “I’ll be back after lunch and some shopping.” Her voice was assertive but her body was Jell-O. She’d convinced herself this was all she needed to do. Just make her plans, be calm, and stick to them. Keith was fragile, didn’t like rejection, but he’d have to understand that she deserved time out too.

Linda was nothing like he was saying. Just like Beth and Renee weren't bad either. He'd found a way to try to keep Marta all to himself. Maybe it was from a place of love or desperation, but either way she couldn't keep it up.

The tirade of curse words nipped at her heels as she closed the car door and drove away. He'd calm down. He'd see she was just taking some well-deserved time to herself. When she got back, they'd talk it out.

But her body never relaxed. She didn't eat her lunch, merely moved it around the plate. Whatever Linda was talking about, it felt as though it were in some foreign language. The shopping they planned next was too much. She'd been gone now for nearly an hour and a half. If Keith was still mad, he'd be simmering in it now.

Feigning a headache, Marta broke away from her plans and drove back home. She'd played out every possible scenario. Maybe he'd ice her out for a few days and then slowly, if she was overcompensating enough, he'd come back around and forgive her. Or he'd be mad, yell, cause a scene but then cool off and by the morning they'd both get over it. The third option was what had her hands shaking. Since they'd gotten married, those yelling fits had turned to something more. She wouldn't admit to even herself that it was abuse. It wasn't punches to the face and black eyes. Just squeezed arms and hard shoves. A handful of hair and a tight grip on her chin so she'd look him in the eyes. He'd shake her, but just to get hold of the situation. And the worse was when he'd hold her down. There was no scarier feeling than being restrained under the guise of getting her to calm down. The feeling of being powerless under his grip still haunted her. To stop the spiraling, she prayed this wouldn't be one of those times.

But she should have been more specific in her prayer. It wasn't any of those three scenarios waiting for her at home. It was far worse.

The curtains were drawn and all the lights off. Everything was exactly as she left it. She knew Keith was home. His truck was in the driveway. The door was unlocked. He wouldn't leave with it open. People couldn't be trusted.

"Keith?" She moved from room to room flipping on lights and pulling open the curtains. He did this sometimes. Made it dark to match his mood. "Where are you?"

The fact that he hadn't answered wasn't much of a surprise to her. Keith didn't like to make things easy. Not when he felt he'd been wronged.

"I know you're home," she called out, not masking her annoyance. She swung between the idea that he was completely out of line and the thought that maybe she'd been insensitive to his feelings.

When she stepped into the bedroom, she saw him slumped on their bed. The lights were off but he hadn't been able to completely block out the afternoon sun coming in from the corners of the blinds.

"Keith, I came home. I skipped shopping and left early. That's what you wanted, right?" She shrugged and waited to read the temperature—how hot he was running. Would he ice her out or burn it all down?

"I can't do this anymore," Keith uttered somberly. "I just can't."

"We don't have to make a big thing out of this," Marta pleaded. "Really. I'm home. It's done."

"You're so selfish," he slurred, and she realized he'd spent the time she was gone very quickly getting wasted. He'd likely skipped the mix and just taken shots straight from a bottle.

"I'm home now." She'd become skilled in keeping herself even and calm. Stating facts rather than emotions.

"I've listened to every story, all your complaining about your mother and what a monster she is. How screwed up your family is. Do you ever wonder if maybe you're the common denominator in all this?" He barely looked up as he spouted his clearly rehearsed speech. The problem wasn't that he was wrong, she wondered quite often about the same thing. He was, in fact, reading out loud the mental diary she kept. And his accusation only made it all the more real.

"We don't need to do this," she repeated flatly. "I get it. It's over."

"You didn't survive your mother," he hissed. "You became her. Doing what you want. To hell with how other people feel. I can't do it anymore. Do you realize I didn't used to be like this?"

Marta wasn't sure if that was true or not, but Keith said it after each of their fights. He was more emphatic if the fight was physical.

"You push me in a way I've never dealt with before. I

didn't used to fly off the handle. But you make me absolutely crazy. I hate it. I don't want to be like this." He waved his hand in the air, and finally she saw it.

Because he had a felony on his record from a bar fight gone wrong, he had her buy the gun. The world was a dangerous place and his paranoia had him constantly on edge. The gun was just going to be something to make him feel more confident about protecting the house. Now as he clutched it tightly in his hand, she understood that was a lie. It would be one more tool to keep the power in his hands.

"Put that down," she said in a shrill and urgent voice. "It was just lunch. It's not that big of a deal. You go out with your friends all the time."

His eyes flashed with anger. "You and I are very different people," he jeered. "You don't think." With that, he put the gun to his temple and banged it twice. "You never think. I can handle myself when I go out. I know what the world is like. You never think." He hit his temple with the gun again.

"Stop pointing that at yourself," she said, her eyes filling with tears. She didn't fear for herself even though past behavior indicated she should. The thought that he might hurt himself was unbearable.

"How many people in your orbit have to die before you realize you're the problem? Your brother. Your father. I stood by you when the whole town was blaming you for his death. People would come up to me and talk about how you killed your dad and I would defend you. Don't you wonder why it keeps happening?"

Again, she couldn't argue. She did wonder this often. "I'm sorry, Keith. Just put the gun away and it's over. It won't happen again."

"You don't want to face it." He laughed humorlessly, his eyes still angry. "You don't want to admit you're the problem. You want to sit with Linda and tell her how I hurt you and I'm a monster. You want to divorce me and tell everyone how bad I am."

"No," Marta implored. "I didn't say anything to Linda. We don't talk about that kind of stuff. It was just lunch. She droned on about her job and her boss. It was nothing."

"You want a divorce. You want to leave me." His voice cracked with emotion.

"I don't," Marta assured him. "I am not going anywhere. I'll be better. I promise I will. I shouldn't have walked out today. I don't know why I did." Her eyes were fixed on the gun.

"You stormed out and slammed the door in my face," he corrected, though she knew that wasn't true. "You just push me so far. I don't know why you have to be like this."

"You're right," she agreed quietly. "Give me the gun. Let's stop this and I promise I won't do anything like that again."

"You drive me insane," he said, tears filling his eyes. "This is not who I am. I don't do things like this."

"I know," she said, reaching her hand out for the gun. "I'm so sorry."

He dropped his hand down into hers, the heavy gun on her palm. She held it like a bomb that might go off. When he sobbed, she ached for him. For what she'd inflicted on this man she said she loved. Someone who'd given her a better shot at life than she'd have had on her own. Sliding open her sock drawer, she put the gun down and made her way back to him. Why was she so toxic? How did her very presence burden people so deeply?

There were many moments she'd watched her mom flail on the floor and pull at her own hair wildly. Her father had been deeply depressed. Her brother drove a car at top speed to flee their madness and lost his life because of it. Now, this man who'd vowed to take care of her was falling to pieces. She was a poison. He was right.

15

Marta

When he was showered and looking fresh, Terrance met her back in the lobby. His cheer was polar opposite to her trepidation. Rather than being happy for the dichotomy of their feelings, she worried for him. He'd be so disappointed to find out just how bad this could be. Fleeing Dreven and starting a new life had been more than self-preservation. It had seemed to save people from her too. Now that she was back in the area, she felt like a landmine anyone could accidently step on.

"Did your mom agree to come out?" His smile was wide and hopeful.

"She did," Marta informed him stoically. "You shouldn't look so happy about it."

"Don't underestimate my charm." He dusted his shoulder off playfully.

"Don't overestimate her sanity." Marta rolled her eyes and drew in a deep breath as they headed back to the parking garage. From the moment she knew Terrance was flying out to help her, she tried to figure out how to have this next conversation. "Can I be honest with you about something?"

"I hope you'll be honest with me about everything."

She shrugged and thought of a way to explain what she felt so he'd understand. "Last night I had a close call with Keith."

Terrance stopped abruptly and faced her. "A close call, what does that mean? Did something happen?"

His posture, the look of concern on his face, made her certain he needed to hear this. "I had walked into a place and someone there told me I'd just missed him. I can't explain what that felt like. The overwhelming feeling of dread. It made me realize if you and I are going to be in town, there's a chance we'll run into him."

"I hope we do," Terrance replied stiffly. "I'm here now. You're not going to have to worry about him." He looked earnestly at her, but that was the reaction she was worried about.

"I need you to promise that when the inevitable happens and we cross paths with him, please don't puff out your chest and feel like you need to defend me."

"That's a pretty difficult promise to keep," he admitted, his head dropping down. "You've told me very little about him, but enough for me to know he doesn't deserve to be within a hundred feet of you. And if he thinks he's going to try anything—"

"I wasn't perfect in our marriage either," she began, swallowing hard. "I used to do things that would drive him nuts."

"No one deserves to deal with abuse at any time. There are no qualifying circumstances that make it okay. Please don't ask me to see his perspective. I'm not going to do that. You left. I'm so proud you did. I know it isn't easy and I'll never judge how long you stayed or what you had to do to get through it, but I won't let you justify any kind of violence from him." Terrance kept his voice level and his face gentle. "I can't promise I'll sit quietly by if he's a problem."

She nodded, grateful for the reminder. "You're right. Maybe I'm just afraid. The more I tell you, the more you'll want to hurt him back. And I know him well enough to know how bad that will end. Keith is not some small problem to solve. Maybe you are under the impression he crossed the line in our marriage and I stood up and left him. I didn't march out, asserting my strength and telling him he had no power over me. I ran. Now, showing back up here, I'm worried the more you hear the angrier you'll get. I don't need another angry man in the mix."

"I'd like to hear whatever you're willing to tell me and I promise I won't allow that to change my reaction if the time comes to deal with Keith. I'm a grown man and I won't do something that makes life harder for you in the long run. I have self-control. If he needs to be dealt with, I can be tactful. But please talk to me. I want to know what we're dealing with."

Marta thought of the simplest way to explain who Keith could be on a bad day. "In the years since I've left, I've been waiting for someone to knock on my door and tell me he'd finally hurt someone so badly or that he'd killed someone. I figured some detective would be at my door with a horror story and I'd have to tell them exactly how bad it had gotten when we were married. I think about who that next person might be and how I didn't do enough to stop him. I only tried to save my own life."

"You can't put that on yourself." Terrance opened her car door and she gladly became his passenger, her mind buzzing too much to drive.

"I know that logically. But it weighs on me sometimes. There is no way he is somehow magically better. It was so bad, so dark; that doesn't just go away. Unless I really was the cause. He was masterful at his abuse. Keith understood every insecurity I had, and it became impossible to consider leaving him. He learned quickly that threatening to harm himself was very impactful to me. That gun to his head was more of a deterrent than when it was pointed at my own head."

"Gun?" Terrance asked, his brows crushing together in concern. "He pointed a gun at you?"

"Yes, but like I said, more often at himself. The threats were endless and effective. I shrank down every aspect of my life until he had nothing to worry about. I was where he wanted when he wanted and continually promised never to leave him. And I was so good at protecting his reputation and making excuses for him that people believed he was the perfect man. I built my own prison, locked myself in, and gave him the key."

"I don't understand how people don't see him for who he is. A guy like that must have a temper with other people too."

"Around here, he's just another tough guy. There's a lot of bravado and drunken arguments when the bar closes. But Keith is reliable. He's a hard worker. Pretty faithful as far as I know. The way people are measured around here, he's one of the better ones."

"He's an abuser."

"I know." Marta rubbed a couple fingers to her temple. "It was so confusing. I really never thought I'd find myself in that situation. I know running probably doesn't seem like the most adult way to handle things but I needed to go."

"How did you finally get out?"

"Do you know abuse is a cycle? It's blow-ups and honeymoon periods and round and round. During the blow-ups, everything is moving so fast. Spinning like a merry-go-round and you can't jump off. In the honeymoon period, things slow down. I eventually figured out that leaving when he was teetering on the edge of violence, leaving when he'd just given me the perfect reason to, wasn't ever going to work. One of us would end up dead."

Terrance put his hand over his heart as if he'd just been wounded by her words.

"It wasn't some big epiphany or long, drawn-out strategy. It was just before Christmas. The only plans we had were the ones he'd made for us. In the summer, I'd started thinking about the fact that I didn't have access to money to buy gifts without asking him. I never had my name on a joint account until the last year of our marriage. Before that I didn't have my own debit card. I took his on days when I needed to buy something. He said it was because it was easier for him to keep the budget balanced if there was only one card being used. Purchases were all discussed ahead of time. So I started putting a little bit of cash away each week for Christmas gifts. I could only put away twenty or so at first, but it was adding up. I put away every penny I could. Then I realized I had enough to go if I wanted to. I could get in my car and survive off this long enough to get a job and find a place to live. It was a sudden sense of freedom I hadn't felt in a long time."

"You were working, though." Terrance looked perplexed. "What was he doing with your money?"

"He managed the money," she said, knowing it wasn't much of an explanation. "He had control. But then all of the sudden I had this money he didn't know about, and right then, things were good between us. It had been a week since his last blow-up. So without much thought, I packed my bags and snuck away when the flowers he'd bought to beg my forgiveness were still in full bloom."

"Did you tell anyone you were going? Did you know where you'd end up?" His lips pursed with worry as if she were still a broke kid in a new town.

"There weren't many people left in my life at that point. Louis, the police officer who helped me, knew I was leaving. He knew my brother; we all grew up together. I begged him to keep it all quiet and he did what he could to walk the line between keeping me safe and keeping it low key. I made him promise not to tell my brother what happened. I just wanted it all to be over. I can't tell you how many times I almost left and didn't. How many times I swore it was over and then caved. But one day I just knew. I called my boss and told him I wouldn't be back. I drove. Kept to myself. It wasn't easy from there. We had a divorce to settle. I didn't ask for anything. I felt lucky to get away with my life; I didn't need the spare room television. Everything had to be done through a third party since I'd filed restraining orders and there was a documented history of abuse. For the first few months, through the lawyer, he wanted to find me and begged me to come back. But eventually, he only wanted to make sure I didn't tell everyone what happened. His obsessiveness faded, or maybe was hitched to someone else by then. All I had to do was shut up and stay away. It was this unwritten contract between us. I could start over as long as I didn't make any problems for him."

"And now here you are about to bring the whole world to town and possibly make plenty of problems for him."

"Right," Marta sighed. "And there is no way that secret will stay buried. My brother knows now. There are a few other people who helped me during that time who I am sure will eventually speak up. Keith is all about perception.

Controlling it. If I take that from him, there'll be a war. It's not just him threatening to hurt me. He'll try to destroy this opportunity. And if history is any indication, he'll threaten to hurt himself too. I don't do well with that."

Terrance nodded as he pulled the car out of the garage and onto the street. "And just bumping into him on the street isn't going to be a very tactful way to handle this." He was starting to understand. If he first assumed some tough words to try to compel her ex to back off would work, he could see now it was much bigger than that.

"But it's almost inevitable. He's going to know I'm back here. He'll hear about it soon enough if he hasn't already. I'm not prepared. And while you might think a fistfight on a street corner in Dreven could solve this whole thing, it'll only make it worse. I just wanted you to understand what we're dealing with."

He hummed and looked thoughtfully down the road. "How did someone like you end up with someone like Keith?"

"We're perfectly matched, actually." She fiddled with her fingers as she thought of their relationship. "Keith was more than my husband. I hadn't lived hardly at all before him. No one got me ready for the world. I had a boyfriend named Eddy before him and he was sweet. He helped with plenty but I still was a kid. When I ended up with Keith there were so many things I didn't know. He raised me, as twisted as that sounds. And having that power, the control over what I learned and how I saw the world, he was able to convince me of just about anything. Including the fact that I had poor judgment. That I couldn't trust my own thoughts. He called me impulsive, and maybe I was a little, but not the way he blew it up. Keith was very good at making the outside world seem so dangerous that the threat he posed was less. I didn't reluctantly fall into a relationship with him. I ran as fast as I could to him. He was older. Had a good job. A place to live. He knew things. He was strong, mentally and physically. I had these dangerous toxic people swarming me my whole life, and he was the first person I'd ever met that I thought could protect me from them. My first boyfriend Eddy was a good guy but he couldn't really deal with all the baggage I had. Keith was a damaged, dangerous man but when he wasn't he took care of me. Imagine how confusing that is."

Terrance kept his gaze ahead, only glancing a time or two at the GPS to make sure he was heading the right way. "It's so strange to hear you talk like this. You are a strong, independent woman and I can't imagine you ending up in that position."

"It's taken a lot of work over the last couple years. Meeting Heather and Ray, starting over in a place I felt safe, that's what changed for me. But I haven't really put it all together yet. The *why*, the *how to stop it from happening again*. I still hear his voice telling me I make bad choices. I'm too naïve. I'm no match for the real world. I need him or I'll never survive."

"Look how well you're doing without him." Terrance put his hand on her knee. "You're on the brink of something amazing. The book you wrote is all you. He had nothing to do with that."

"And yet my entire future still hangs in the balance. He still has the power. When he hears there will be attention coming my way, when he considers what that might mean for him, he'll try everything to destroy it. And there's a long line of people willing to help him. My mother is a disaster. My father's side of the family blames me for his death. And now Keith will do whatever it takes to keep his abuse a secret."

"Well, I agree, it's not going to be very straightforward—"

"Please tell me the last scandal for a recipient of this award. What was the last bit of damage control someone needed to do on your end?" She smirked, knowing the answer would be comical.

"I did hear about six years ago one of the people in the running for the award lied about being in a fraternity. Apparently, he'd never made it through rush week."

"Say it isn't so," she gasped playfully. "What a disgrace. How was it handled?"

"He wasn't selected for the award so it didn't matter. If he had been and it came out after, there would have been swift damage control and we'd just wait until the next buzz item on the news cycle. It's not that different than middle school. When something bad happens to you, the best thing to do is keep your head down and wait for someone to trip in the cafeteria and land in their own mashed potatoes."

"I have a feeling it won't be that easy."

"This conversation certainly has me questioning my original tactics," Terrance admitted. "I was looking forward to bumping into Keith and letting him know he should stay out of your way. A few poorly veiled threats and maybe a punch to the throat. We're going to need a new strategy."

"You can save that tactic for my mom at lunch today. It might work on her."

Terrance laughed, gripping the steering wheel tightly. "I'm not throat punching your mother. I told you, it's my charm that will win her over. She'll be your biggest cheerleader when I'm done with her."

"I'll bite my tongue with the 'I told you so' speech when we're leaving lunch."

"Same." He winked and she melted. Though the circumstances were complete garbage, she was relieved to have him near.

16

Carol

Carol felt like she should be dressed in some clandestine outfit and start skulking through her own childhood home. Lying wasn't part of her normal routine, but she knew the people in her life would work hard to stop her if she told the truth about what she was doing tonight. They'd be well-intentioned and probably right, but she'd already made up her mind. Carol had a blind date with the past.

Her mother's journals smelled of her familiar perfume mixed with the musk of the attic. They were precisely labeled and all the same brand and style. She'd likely ordered the leather-bound books from an overseas boutique. Not because there wasn't something just as beautiful close by. Francine loved to utter the word *imported* every chance she got.

With a glass of red wine poured nearly to the top and salmon from her favorite restaurant, Carol readied for the pain. There was now a reason, an important business strategy at play. That's what she kept telling herself. It was her duty to try to find out what Eli knew about her father. If she could get some kind of insight, she'd have the advantage. Surely whatever the secret was, her mother would have known about it and written it down. She loved to keep an inventory of people's mistakes. It made throwing them in their faces as easy as checking an old receipt.

Carol was bracing for the worst. Her father was human and in a seemingly loveless, sometimes hostile marriage. Maybe he'd strayed. Eli was in the same circles as him; there was a chance he'd heard or even seen something that would sully her father's reputation. But claiming he had some irrefutable proof was a different story.

It was foolish to think her father was perfect, though she had harbored that belief for most of her life. When she'd stepped into the business world full-time and gotten an up-close and personal look at men in power, she realized if he was without faults, he'd be the only one.

All of this would be easier if it was the only thing on her mind. Not hearing a positive update from Terrance was yanking at the other half of her brain, tug-of-war style. There had been high stakes in her life before, but this certainly felt like a make-or-break moment all around.

The first entry in the first journal was dated a few months after Carol was born. She imagined there were other journals somewhere from before her mother was married. It would be very much like her to keep them all separated. Too afraid to invest heavily in the words, she merely skimmed the text. It was flowery and upbeat. Francine spoke of Carol and motherhood in a dreamy sort of way. A lifelong goal fulfilled. By all accounts, Carol was perfect. A good sleeper. Charming when company came over, even at three months old. The few mentions of Dallas were also positive. Though he was working long hours, trying to establish himself in the company, when he was home, all his attention was on his girls.

Carol flipped through a few more sections of the journal, and it was much the same. A happy mother, a cherished time, a perfect baby. The neat, familiar penmanship and perfectly spaced and dated entries showed her mother's personality perfectly. Even books meant only for herself to read had to be perfect. Getting to the end of that journal brought her to about age three. Uneventful ramblings about toddler milestones, handmade dresses, and a cheery disposition.

The next book started out with the same tone and Carol was certain this would prove fruitless. Her mother was perhaps writing with the hope someone would read these someday. This would be a performative piece. Revisionist history that scrubbed out all the uncomfortable parts and left only shiny, happy people.

There was an abrupt shift in the handwriting by the

middle of the second journal. The margins were scribbled in. The words slanting.

I am at my wits end. This child refuses to obey. For the third time in a row, she's embarrassed me at tea. No matter how much I scold her, she continues to fidget and fuss. It was a full-on tantrum when I wouldn't let her have another scone. She's already two sizes bigger than she should be at her age. The only saving grace is she's scheduled to get her tonsils out in three weeks and at least then she'll have a chance to lose some of what she's gained these last six months. Her doctor said he is not concerned about her weight but he is not the one trying to raise a proper young lady.

Dallas is no help at all. Always indulging her and allowing the most outlandish forms of pretend and play. Carol has failed at ballet, violin, and can hardly sit for tea without pulling her dress up over her head. To have the burden of only one child and for it to be this child is almost more than I can bear. She was once my agreeable baby doll but now she has a mind of her own.

Carol burst out laughing. The connotation that having a mind of her own was some kind of curse, a plague set upon her mother. The entire passage made her both sad and proud. She'd often wondered if she and her mother ever shared a bond. If there had been a time she'd lived up to her mother's expectations. Now she knew there was. From birth to around age four, Carol had been enough. She was affable and obedient. But when the world became bigger and the temptations to test the waters became too great, Carol could not remain her mother's little doll.

She didn't recall with much clarity the teas she ruined or the ballet classes she'd been too unruly to finish. But she did recall her mother's cool demeanor in public and harsh words in private. This was the year her mother stopped loving her. Maybe not fully, but at least stopped loving her unconditionally. From this point on there were strings attached. If Carol wanted affection or approval from her mother, it was only in exchange for proper behavior. This was validation of how it all began, yet she didn't feel satisfied at all. Flipping forward, she skimmed the rest of that book and found more of the same. Complaints about Carol's shortcomings and growing frustration with Dallas for not being harder on her.

Now Carol felt as though she could easily sort out what each subsequent book might say. From toddler to teen, she knew every disappointing thing she'd done in her mother's eyes. They'd all be cataloged here. If her goal was to learn about something her father might have been hiding, she couldn't allow herself to wade aimlessly through her mother's diatribe of dissatisfaction.

There was a catharsis to seeing it all laid out so neatly. It was Carol's fall from grace, step by step. From her distracting love of books to her fluctuating weight, in Francine's eyes her daughter was deliberately failing to meet the standard of their family. Tossing another book back onto the stack, she shoved the box to the side. When the bottom shifted, it revealed more space below the journals. A compartment that could easily be missed.

Carol yanked the rest of the useless journals out and tossed them unceremoniously onto the floor. It felt good to mix up their order and maybe dent their pristine bindings. When the chest was empty, she shifted the false bottom out of the way and revealed two more books. They didn't match each other or the set she'd just gone through. They were plain brown leather with an attached silk bookmark tucked inside.

The thought crossed her mind that they might belong to her father. His words, the inner workings of his mind, would be a true treasure to discover. Dallas had willpower and the ability to bite his tongue. No matter how bad the situation became, he never really spoke poorly of Francine. Perhaps in these journals he would have. But quickly, when she opened the first one, she realized these two belonged to her mother. Dated earlier than the others. Not quite as frequently written in, they seemed to span more than two years in each thin book. She calculated when her parents were married and realized these would predate that by a year or two. Their courtship years. The great mystery of her life had been how her parents ever ended up with each other. Were they different people then or equally incompatible but somehow resigned to marriage? She sometimes wondered if her mother had gotten pregnant and marriage then became mandatory. But that math didn't work out.

The courtship was documented with little hearts over some letters and as punctuation. Different colored pens ranging from purple to green separated each entry. Her mother would have been just over twenty. Every page of the first book was oozing with happiness. The second book was all in blue pen. Splotches Carol assumed were teardrops fell sporadically on different pages. Her parents were not yet married by this time, but clearly something had changed. As she skimmed the pages, she saw it. The truth she was so afraid to find. One far worse than she imagined. Eli had been right. This would demolish her father's legacy. If exploited enough, it could even tarnish her own.

Closing the book like she had trapped a spell inside, she tossed it to the floor. There would be no peace until she read each page and understood exactly what she was dealing with.

When her phone rang, she jumped and fished it clumsily out of her pocket.

"Hello?" she huffed, a cool chill running up her spine.

"Is everything all right?" Robert asked, sounding vexed. "Where are you?"

"I'm at my parents' estate. Sorting through old things."

"That sounds miserable. Wait," he groaned knowingly. "Are you reading the journals? You know that's nothing but trouble."

"I had to find out if there was anything in them about my father and what Eli might know."

"You're playing with fire," he said sweetly, clearly worried by the tone of her voice. "Nothing good can come of that."

"Playing with fire," she sighed in agreement. "I think I've gotten burned."

"Send me the address; I'll come over." Robert didn't leave room for debate, but she knew she had to try anyway.

"It's late. That's not a good idea. We're already pressing our luck with lunch meetings. People will start talking. Eli will look for any reason to undermine me." She rambled, listing all the reasons he shouldn't come as she wished deeply he still would.

"Too bad," he replied quickly. "You shouldn't be there alone digging up the past. It's not good. Let me come by and you can get a fresh perspective. Maybe it's not as bad as you think."

She chuckled at the absurdity. "It's pretty bad."

Robert stayed silent for a long beat. "Carol, send me the address. Let me come over. No one is going to know. I don't want you to be alone." He paused and corrected himself. "I want to be with you."

She nodded, knowing he couldn't see her, but she needed more time to blink away her tears and settle her voice. "Why does this have to be so complicated?"

"Our parents aren't infallible. Relationships can be really complex."

"I don't just mean my parents. Look at what I'm trying to do. Look at why I'm up here. It's a game of chess. I have to convince Marta she's safe and worthy. I have to convince my peers now is the time to change things in our industry. I have to fend off men like Eli who are entrenched in their own superiority. Now I have to contend with my father's failures and faults. All in the name of making space for people who deserve long-overdue opportunities. My options are to quietly take what I'm given and keep things exactly how they've always been or take on the world. There's no middle ground. No baby steps that actually drive change. I have to be persistent and faultless."

"One misstep and you'll lose the chance," Robert said, shocking her with his agreement. "It's not fair and it's not just, but it's important work. I think your father put your future in motion so you could find yourself right where you are today. It wasn't only about making his daughter a success."

"You're right," she nodded again, clutching her phone tighter. "I know he wanted better for people. He knew I could be the catalyst for that."

"And I'm sure he knew you could take it when things got hard. What would he tell you right now if he were there?"

Carol looked down at the journals and then the jewelry on her hand and laughed. She was standing in the attic of her parents' multimillion-dollar estate. One of the rings she was wearing was worth a fortune. Her father's words echoed through her soul. She could practically hear his advice. "He would tell me I'm being self-indulgent. There is a whole world of people who would trade anything to be in this hard spot I'm in. And the livelihoods on the line right now are much more at risk than my own. I'm never going to go without. I'm set for life. If I'm ousted as the CEO and I fail to change anything, only my pride will take a hit." She sniffled as she thought of Marta and Terrance. "But there is a hell of a lot more at risk for everyone else. I've got to keep that in perspective. This sometimes feels fundamentally about me. But it's not. I might have to fall on my sword if it means opening a door for someone else. I've risen to the place I always wanted to be. I'm the one who has to take the risk now."

"I can't imagine there was anything in those journals that could take away from what your father instilled in you."

A pang of regret surged through her as she realized that, on this, Robert was wrong. "Do you want to come over still? You might not be so optimistic once you read them for yourself. Maybe we can find a way to minimize the damage."

"I'll be right there," Robert promised, his sincerity enveloping her like a hug. "But attics freak me out. Can we do this in the kitchen or something?"

"I'll have some tea waiting," Carol chuckled. "I used to be a hellion at tea time. It drove my mother crazy. I've got the proof in her own handwriting."

"I'm famous for bumping the table and plunking the sugar cubes in too clumsily. Your mother wouldn't have approved of me either."

Carol thought about that for a moment. "My mother would have adored you," she admitted hesitantly. "It's probably why I wouldn't have dated you while she was alive. I never wanted to give her the satisfaction that maybe she was right."

"Right about which part?"

"That there were good men with kind smiles who could also be successful and faithful. That a woman could want her own career and loyal companionship. I told her I had to choose and she reminded me often that I chose wrong. You'd have been the unicorn she wanted me to find."

"Until she saw me pour tea," he said, levity breaking the unbearable heaviness of the moment.

"You're charming enough to get away with it. Now hurry up and get here so you can talk me off the ledge yet again."

"You're never really on the ledge," Robert quipped earnestly. "You've always got it under control. But I like to be useful, so I'll come and pretend you need me."

"People can't know," she whispered as though the walls had ears. "I can't afford a scandal right now. I seem to be on the brink of plenty of my own."

"No one needs to know anything. It shouldn't be scandalous for us to be there for each other. But if it is, then we keep it just between us. Well, us and the ghosts in what I'm assuming is your mother's haunted attic."

17

Marta

It smelled of roast chicken and deep-fryer grease, yet the nostalgia was unmistakable and inviting. Marta's mother worked at The Paulus Roast Chicken Restaurant for a couple years as a waitress. The family-style chicken dinner was famous. Or at least within a ten-mile radius. Anything classified as bottomless or all-you-can-eat was a popular favorite in the area. There were perks that came with working in food service. After school, the bus would drop Marta and her brothers off close by and they'd wait for their mother to finish her shift. On good days they'd behave well enough and finish their homework in a corner booth. This would result in a basket of fries or whatever leftover food the kitchen could spare.

The bad days were different. They were children. Rambunctious from a full day of school. Bored with having to wait for their mother to finish work. They'd act out, and she would verbally annihilate them into submission. They'd be left smelling the food that ended up on tables right near them and coveting every bite they didn't get to take. Like most things in her past, she had pebbles of joy and boulders of trauma.

"I tried to warn you," she said quietly over her shoulder to Terrance. They were making their way toward a booth where her mother had already set up shop. Her oversized purse was splayed across the table, keys with too many key chains clanking around.

"No apologies," he reminded her. "We've got this."

"Over here," her mother bit out, curtly waving them toward the table.

"I know, Mom, I could hear your keys banging on the table when we walked in the door." She rolled her eyes at the rabbit's foot and bottle openers hanging off the lanyard in her mother's hand. Why she carried all that around was still a mystery.

"Pardon my existence," Wendy sighed, tucking her keys dramatically into her bag. "And am I going to have to hear about how you wanted to eat somewhere else too? Nothing is good enough for you anymore."

"This place looks perfect," Terrance chimed in. "It's nice to meet you." She took his extended hand and smiled. Attention was impossible for her to pass up.

"Oh, at least you brought someone with manners," Wendy cooed, gesturing for Terrance to sit.

"You used to work here, right?" Terrance asked, keeping his eyes fixed on Wendy and looking unabashedly intrigued by her pending answer. To Marta, it was part nauseating and part wonderful. Terrance already recognized exactly what he'd need to do to win Wendy over.

"I did," Wendy said, her chin tipping up with pride, though Marta couldn't for the life of her understand why. "These kids will tell you they went without, but it's bull."

Marta opened her mouth to snipe back, but Terrance gently rested his hand on her leg under the table. A clear *I got this* signal.

"Judging by Marta's writing and what I know of her so far, she must have come by that talent and charm somewhere." He flashed that smile and the impossible-to-resist, dimple-framed grin that would make even the most hardened heart melt.

Wendy was falling for it—hook, line, and sinker—but couldn't let the compliment of Marta stand unanswered. "Don't get too attached to this one," she said pointedly, gesturing with her chin to Marta. "This girl doesn't know how to hold on to a good man. I thought I had her married off and out of my hair, and she blew it."

Terrance had a hell of a poker face, but he faltered. Clearing his throat, he tried to right himself quickly. "Did Marta tell you about the opportunity she has—?"

"The *award*?" Wendy asked, throwing up condescending air quotes. "You know why they picked her, right?"

"I do," Terrance replied through a wide smile. "I actually had a hand in the selection, so I had a front-row seat to the process. Marta's writing is so compelling and spellbinding really."

"She's a pity pick," Wendy snickered. "You don't have to try to sell me on it. That's the way of the world right now. Find some underprivileged soul and toss them a bone. It makes your company look good."

Terrance shifted his posture. Not nervously, but to show he was serious. "That's not the case at all. I won't sit here and speak for the entire foundation I work for. But I can unequivocally say that Marta won this award on the merit of her work."

Wendy only hummed and rolled her eyes. "If you say so. I believe my daughter is talented, don't get me wrong. I just don't think a place like that comes looking for a girl like her unless they have an agenda."

Terrance blinked slowly at her and kept his voice serious. "The agenda is to cultivate and highlight the top talent in each category of the arts. Of all the novels published last year, hers stood out."

"And she makes for a good story too? Rags to riches?" Wendy looked abundantly pleased with herself, which only irritated Marta further. Terrance, however, looked unflappable.

"A good story?" He chuckled. "How's that working out so far? She nearly turned down the award to avoid having to tell any part of her story. As a matter of fact, she hasn't signed the contract yet. My boss is a brilliant woman. She knows there are far less complicated situations out there. Recipients who could breeze right through the process. And nothing is even locked in yet with Marta."

There was a flash of worry on Wendy's face, but she fought it back. She instead busied herself with the menu she knew by heart. "You haven't signed the contract?" she asked point-blank. "Why not?"

Terrance answered for her. "You're one reason. Marta has enough to contend with when it comes to stepping into the inevitable spotlight coming her way. The least of her worries should be what her mother has to say when the cameras turn on or the newspapers start calling."

"I never said—"

"Your daughter is this close"—he held up his fingers pinched just an inch apart—"to having a shot at success. The kind that opens every door and gets rid of all the bullshit little problems that come from never having enough of anything. Whether you're happy for her or not, whether you care about her career or not, the smart move would be to get on board now. And you strike me as a smart woman." He paused for a moment but didn't give either of them enough time to speak. "All you need to do is either come up with something supportive to say about Marta, defend her if the time comes, or shut your mouth and keep to yourself."

"What makes you think I care about her suddenly getting rich and famous?" Wendy snapped, but the real bite was gone from her voice. The wheels in her mind were churning quickly.

"You'd be a fool not to. Maybe this is your favorite restaurant. Maybe you wouldn't change a thing about your life. But you've been around long enough to know it doesn't take much to strip away what you have. You can always have less. Something catastrophic can be right around the corner. Then what? What safety net do you have anymore? This, what's being asked of you, takes very little effort and it has the potential for enormous reward. Take it."

Wendy looked at Marta expectantly. "You're not going to say anything for yourself?"

Marta shrugged. "I think he covered it. Really, it's your choice. Be on my side, or be alone. At least on my side, we have a shot at something better. Glenn is about to start his own family. He's not going to have time or money to come keep your house standing. It's falling apart around you."

"And I'm supposed to believe you'll just take care of it all? You have a bad habit of running away."

Marta placed her palm firmly on the table and leaned in toward her mother. "I only run when there is something I need to get away from. Don't give me a reason."

"Fine," Wendy said, twisting her mouth up as if she'd tasted something sour. "Whatever. I'll be supportive. I'll behave for the cameras. But I want assurances that you're not going to just abandon me when you get everything you want. You are your father's daughter. I'm sure you inherited that from him."

"It's good you brought up assurances," Terrance said,

reaching into his shoulder bag and pulling out some documents. "These are non-disclosure agreements. Legally binding documents that outline exactly what will happen if you decide to slander, undermine, or otherwise tarnish Marta's character in any way. In return for that, there will be a stipend provided for your basic needs. Something to ensure that you remain comfortable while you remain quiet." He slid the papers and a serious-looking pen over to her.

"I'm not signing anything," Wendy scoffed and again fixed her eyes on Marta. She wouldn't give her mother the satisfaction of seeming surprised by this play Terrance was making.

Instead, she looked her mother dead in the eyes as she spoke. "You're either with me or against me, Mom. Maybe that's always been the case, but this time there's more on the line for you to lose besides just a daughter. Maybe I've been expendable in the past, but you're not deciding about what kind of relationship you want with me. You're deciding if you can swallow your feelings long enough to realize this is what's best for all of us. It's your choice." Marta gestured with her chin at the documents sitting in front of her mother.

"What are you going to tell the world about me? I don't have some fancy boyfriend to write up documents to keep you quiet."

"I'll tell the world the truth," Marta said, her voice softer now. "My parents did the best they could with what they had. Even through unbearable loss and constant compounding hardships, we've managed to make it this far.

It wasn't perfect, but it was perfectly designed to get me right where I am today." She folded her hands neatly and placed them in her lap.

The loudest silence fell between them. Leaving her mother speechless was a rare accomplishment. Terrance clearly knew enough to let the moment stand uninterrupted.

Without a word, her mother took the pen, examined the papers superficially, and then signed them.

"Thank you," Marta whispered, relief flooding her body.

"Don't thank me. I gave you everything. I worked myself half to death in places like this just to end up with coin tips, stained clothes, and hurting feet. You would think you'd want to say more about me than that. But I'm sure you'll have something shining to say about your father."

"I plan to say the least I possibly can about anyone, to be honest," Marta replied firmly. "None of this is idyllic fairy tale stuff. I know who we are, I know where we come from."

"I don't want much to do with this," Wendy replied coolly. "I'm not getting dressed up or pretending to be something I'm not. I won't run around and tell people all the trouble you caused me, but likewise, I don't plan to paint some fake rosy picture. Just leave me out of all this. Maybe you've decided you're willing to be used by these people to make themselves look good. You can deal with the fallout on your own."

"Or maybe it'll be life-altering and amazing," Marta challenged, hardly believing the words herself.

"It's all been garbage. Nothing goes our way, and when

it does, we blow it. That's the kind of people we are and the place we're from. You're not going to outrun that."

Terrance slid the paper back toward himself and cleared his throat. "You've been dealt some bad hands. But eventually, the luck has to turn."

"No," Wendy replied, leaning back against the booth. "Most of us die well before that happens. I want what's coming to me from all this. That stipend or whatever but then keep out of my business."

Terrance nodded, looking very pleased with the outcome. "There will be a point person to deal with all press. We can help you find tactful ways to turn down interviews and establish the fact with the press that you're a very private person. After losing your son and the father of your children so tragically, you've worked hard to find peace. People will understand being protective of that."

Wendy sneered. "You better be careful bringing up my dead ex-husband with any press. Marta told you what happened, right? Half the town will line up to tell the story to whoever will print it."

"We'll deal with that," Terrance replied confidently. "That's not your concern now."

"Devil's tongue," Wendy said, pointing at Terrance but staring at Marta. "This man is trouble. Too slick for his own good. I was warning the wrong person when you two sat down. It's you, girl, who needs to watch out."

"I can handle myself," Marta replied, a chill running up her spine. There had been something effortless about Terrance's balance of threats and persuasion. She knew nothing about these non-disclosure documents or the tactic he planned to use at lunch.

It worked. Wasn't that what mattered? Her mother would now be quiet, keep to herself, and not go out of her way to make Marta look bad. That was an enormous win. The consequences would be large enough now that Wendy would not dare breach the contract. The cash she'd get could keep her quiet.

Wendy got up, groaning and wincing in pain. "I need pills, so I'm not waiting long for that money. That's what happens when you beat your body up working to feed your ungrateful children. You have pain."

"Where are you going?" Marta asked, looking confused.

"I'm going up to the kitchen to order my food to go and putting it on your check. Then I'm getting the hell out of here. You want to keep making deals with the devil, be my guest. I'm done."

"Okay." Marta sighed sarcastically. "Bye."

"You should have stayed with Keith," Wendy bit back, leaning heavily on the table as she caught her breath. "I told him you're back here, and I told him about all this business." She waved her hand at Terrance. "If you were smart, you'd get back with him before you sign that contract. He was always the one with the good head on his shoulders. He'd watch out for you. Why you ever wanted to go out into the world on your own like a fool, I'll never understand. It's how you end up with situations like this."

Marta's hands slicked with sweat and her heart thudded against her ribs. "You told him about this?"

Wendy rolled her eyes. "You two were married," she hissed. "He's still my son-in-law as far as I'm concerned, and I thought he should know you were back here and planning to bring all sorts of trouble with you. I can't imagine what you'd have bad to say about him but if you plan to, he deserves to know."

"What did he say?" Marta asked, clutching Terrance's thigh below the table, holding on for dear life.

"That he'd catch up with you about it. Like me, he doesn't exactly like the idea of you putting his life on display for the world. He was not happy." Wendy's smug expression only exacerbated Marta's swirling anxiety. For so long, her primary job was to make sure Keith was happy. Happy equaled safe.

"You shouldn't have told him," Marta said, her eyes fixed ahead on nothing in particular and her voice far off.

Terrance leaned in and whispered. "It'll be okay. We'll handle him too."

Marta closed her eyes and waited until she was certain her mother was gone before opening them again. Gulping back the emotion, she felt an urgency to leave. To run. Terrance's voice was all she could hear.

"Marta, I know this seems impossible. Clearly Keith is something to contend with, but you were alone back then. You were young and had no one. Now you have me."

"Terrance." She leaned her head on his shoulder. "I'm glad you're here but there are some things you can't do."

"Like what? Try me."

"You can't make me bulletproof."

18

Carol

The temptation to get online and do some more in-depth research was compelling, but she fought it off. There was no telling where this might lead, and something like that might matter. If she were to play dumb, it would be important that she didn't leave some electronic trail. That would be a rookie move.

Robert looked worried when he stepped into the large mahogany-paneled foyer and saw her sitting near an elaborate tray of tea and mini sandwiches.

"You don't even live here," he said with a wry smile. "Do you travel with tiny little sandwiches in your bag just in case?"

"No," Carol said, standing and moving closer toward

Robert. She wanted to hug him, to be hugged by him, but she stopped short. "I try to give the small staff here some notice when I'll come by. They are miracle workers and seem to anticipate every need that may arise. I asked for tea and they put out this spread. Sorry you had to drive out here."

"It was a beautiful ride. This estate is magnificent. You were a very lucky child." He looked up at the hand-carved molding and the rare art pieces.

"Yes, every child dreams of drafty rooms and antiques they aren't allowed to touch." She dropped her head bashfully. "But I was lucky to never go without. We always had more than we needed. My father made sure of that."

"He was a hard worker," Robert said, leading Carol to the conversation he seemed to know she needed to have. "And a good man."

"I'm looking at this place differently now," she admitted. "He always tempered my admiration for him with talk of vague failures. I thought he was being modest or humble. There were never any whispers of scandal when it came to my father, and now I know why. The men who would have had the power to expose my father would have been just as culpable. It's not until Eli finds use for the truth as leverage that it becomes viable again."

"What did you find?" Robert asked, stepping in closer to her, an earnest expression on his face. If she were reading the signals right, he too wished they could embrace.

"My mother was crying into her journals. Big teardrops

splotching the ink. Years before I was born, my father was a member of the TRB. Do you know what that is?"

"Sure," Robert said, looking uneasy. "I don't have a breadth of knowledge on it but I've heard of it. A group in the fifties; it kind of went hand in hand with the communist scare and all the blacklisting, right?"

"Same era, yes." Carol took a seat by the tray of tea and poured them each a cup. "How do you take yours?"

"Two sugars please." He sat by her on the tiny couch rather than the safe distance of the wingback chair. Like a teenager sharing popcorn at the movies, she was electrified by the brush of his fingers on hers as she handed over the tea.

"My mother wrote in-depth about the group and its beliefs. It's more than just a blemish on my father's legacy. The TRB was founded in the fifties under the guise of demanding limited government involvement in a wide range of situations. They were adamantly opposed to redistribution of wealth, any kind of government oversight, and staunchly believed that globalization would be the downfall of the United States. Essentially the founding principles were to keep the rich rich, keep the government out of their business, and keep the United States out of all global affairs."

"I would say there is a thread of that that carries through too many people's political beliefs even today," Robert said with a shrug as he sipped his tea and placed it neatly back in the saucer. "At the time, there was a panic about communism and its ability to infiltrate our government. Groups were, of course, formed to combat that."

"Like I said, it was all pretext to be able to create something that would fly under the radar. The real TRB was far more insidious. I studied the group in a college course, never knowing my father was a part of it. They were extremists who published doctrines propagating hate and demonizing every aspect of the world that they didn't directly see themselves reflected in. Everything was made to look like an attack on their success and wealth. Men joined in droves, and the group became a breeding ground for violent protests and dangerous ideology. It was denounced by every political party. When that went public, there was a mass exodus—men leaving the group to distance themselves."

"Do you think there was a chance your father didn't realize what he'd gotten himself into?"

"He was practically a founding member, judging by my mother's journal entry."

Robert leaned back on the couch and looked thoughtfully around the room. "So she was upset when she found out? I expect that could be a shock."

Carol cackled. "Those tear-filled pages were documenting the time when my father decided to leave the TRB. She loved it. Most of her writings were about how stellar the people were and all the opportunities it opened up to my father. She was furious he was leaving. And don't get too excited; it wasn't as if people began denouncing the group and he immediately left. He stayed long enough after that for it to be a problem. There's no way he wouldn't have known what he was involved with. It was a conscious choice."

"I don't—" Robert shook his head. "I've got nothing. Sorry."

"There really isn't anything to say. The only reason this hasn't been exposed yet is because my father didn't have many enemies. People loved him. They rooted for him. It figures that I am the one to make an enemy hostile enough to dig this up."

"What do you imagine would happen if Eli exposed this? Your father is gone. You weren't even born yet. It can't reflect on you."

"Eli can twist things to his benefit. TRB pioneered the idea of lobbying, dumping money into politics in an organized way. Putting pressure on politicians in order to make sure their agenda was always front and center. This was a group based on exclusion and superiority. The only thing that kept it from being labeled as something more sinister was money. And this is where my father got his start. This house was built because my father was given opportunities from powerful men within the TRB. Oh," she groaned as the thought came back to her, "these were staunch misogynists. They touted all sorts of nonsense about women being less qualified and weak. They thought any women in the workforce, besides traditional roles, would go against American values and destroy the family structure. Why would my father align with that and then work so hard to help me have a career?" She put her hand to her head trying to grab hold of the dizzying thought.

"People change. I'm not the same man I was in my twenties. Having daughters, I'll admit, changed me. Maybe your father had some kind of awakening. It seems as though he dedicated much of his time and career in later years to making the companies he was a part of more accessible to everyone."

"Which will look like a complete sham once this comes out." Carol put her untouched tea down and shook her head.

"Well, maybe it won't come out. Eli couldn't care less about your father's legacy. It's only leverage to him. Maybe some negotiation is in order."

"No," Carol said firmly. "I will not play his game. My father made his choices years ago. He built part of his success on the ideals of exclusion, division, and oppression. I will never have the opportunity to ask him why he joined or why he left."

"There wouldn't likely be an answer to satisfy you. Think of your own experiences. Nothing is black or white. Motivation is always more complex than that. I'm not excusing your father's behavior or his association with the TRB. I just don't think you could speculate your way into knowing how it happened or why."

"It's a shame my mother only wrote about his leaving as a negative. She didn't seem to care about any other details. It was all about how his involvement had solidified them as a power couple. Nauseating accounts of whose house the meetings were held at and what type of food was served.

Whether the hostess had properly kept the flow of the evening moving appropriately. The idea that all of that was ending was more painful to her than the notion of why all of it had started in the first place." Carol waved her hands animatedly as she felt the anger at her mother rise to a fever pitch. "I can't believe that even from the grave she's in my head. I couldn't even keep the idealist view of my father safe."

"Your father, as you knew him, is the same man. Maybe he was making amends. Perhaps he was deeply conflicted. But he raised you to be strong and defy everything the TRB stood for. That's real. You don't have to doubt that." Robert's arm enveloped her and she leaned against his chest, the tears flowing freely. He was perfect at this. The precise amount of grip on her arm to make her feel safe. Resting his chin gently on the crown of her head, whispering that it would all be all right.

She leaned in, not just physically to him, but metaphorically. Demolishing the wall of rules that stood between them and stepping over the rubble until there was no space left between them at all. "This is not right," she mumbled, wanting to give him an out if he so desired.

"I've been a good man, Carol." His voice was raspy and low, and she listened with her ear pressed to his chest. "I have followed the rules, been faithful to every commitment I've ever made. And you know what it got me? A divorce and plenty of career ups and downs. I'm this old man trying to remember how to date and learning how to let my children be their own people. I don't hurt anyone. I don't buck the system. But I'm here with you, and if it feels this good to have you in my arms, then what the hell does following the rules get me? This isn't the Boy Scouts; I'm not trying to earn a badge. I'm living my life. The one I've worked hard for. Please don't ask me to let you go right now. I will. I'll always respect what you want, but I'd really like to stay like this until you feel better."

She sniffled and allowed her heart to flutter as she drank in his words and his cologne. "And then what? What happens when I feel better?"

"Then I'd like to kiss you." He squeezed her a bit tighter for a moment.

"And then what?" she pressed, his voice charging her with energy and relief all at once.

"I don't know," he admitted. "Maybe kiss some more, or if it's terrible and you want me to go, I'll probably take a few of these sandwiches. I skipped lunch."

With genuine giddy excitement, she giggled. "You're welcome to the sandwiches, but I don't think I'll ask you to leave."

"You're smiling," he said as she pulled away and gazed into his warm and welcoming eyes. "I was hoping you'd smile."

"And I was hoping you'd kiss me. Maybe we'll both get what we want?" She knew in her mind that Robert was an integral part of her business life and her strategy. His position on the board and the support he'd lend her was crucial. But right now the only position she cared about was the one that had him leaning in and tipping her chin gently toward his.

It was an enduring kiss. Not frenzied or rushed. The dates she'd been on in the last decade, the men she kissed were always in a hurry. Rushed by the expectation of more. She missed the slow burn of a patient man who understood the importance of savoring the moment. Robert kissed her as if they'd held each other a thousand times before.

Brushing her hair back gently, he leaned back and kept his eyes fixed on her. There was an excited wonderment that matched her own sense of eager anticipation. "Should I take a few sandwiches and go?" he asked through a bright, knowing smile.

"Don't go," she begged, taking his hand in hers. "I never break the rules. I always have to be better than average, work twice as hard and make sure I never give anyone a reason to doubt me. It's exhausting. I want a break."

"Maybe breaking a couple of rules together wouldn't be the end of the world," Robert said with a little shrug. "I'm willing to wait around and find out."

19

Marta

"He knows," she stammered, pacing around the hotel lobby. "My mother has no loyalty. Even if I sat there and explained to her how bad things were between Keith and me, she would still find a way to justify it. That's why I've never told her. It's not because I was embarrassed for her to know. It was just completely apparent she wouldn't care."

"We'll sort it out," Terrance said, pulling her into his arms. They hadn't been this close in proximity since their kiss in California, and she'd missed it terribly. Being in his arms was a refuge, something she needed desperately now. "Look how well it went with your mother. I honestly never expected she would quickly sign that non-disclosure agreement. I was expecting she'd negotiate or play hardball."

"My mother lives off a disability check every month and barely has enough to keep her house from falling in around her. Of course she'd take what she could and run." Marta pressed herself closer to him. "It won't work that way with Keith. Money won't matter. He's going to be concerned with his reputation. I've kept all of this to myself for years. No one in this town, besides the few people who helped me get out, ever knew. And they swore not to say anything to anyone because they knew it would only bring more danger to my doorstep."

"If Keith is most worried about people finding out the truth, maybe we can assure him they won't. This is a small town; maybe we can ask the right people and get the restraining orders and police reports buried. Then you can tell Keith you have no intention of breaking your silence. You have a proven track record of keeping this to yourself. With enough assurances and some groundwork, we can put this to rest."

"I guess we're about to find out," Marta said, a lightning bolt of fear zapping through her body. Keith was walking through the revolving door of the hotel, already locking eyes with her. "That's him."

"He's here?" Terrance asked, his arms squeezing just a little tighter around her.

"Don't try to win the battle here," Marta pleaded. "We need to think about the long game, right?" Her voice cracked as he let her go and took a step in front of her.

"I want to lay him out on his ass," he admitted through

gritted teeth. "But I want you to get what you deserve in life more, so I won't."

"Marta," Keith said, overly exaggerating his polite tone. "I talked to your mother. It seems like you and I have some things to discuss."

"I'm Terrace." He jutted his hand out firmly and leaned to block Marta even more. "Why don't we find somewhere we can all talk."

"This doesn't involve you," Keith said, his reddish-brown brows crashing together. "Marta and I have some things to discuss."

"Not happening," Terrance said through a forced smile. "Those things you need to discuss involve me and the company I work for." He gestured to a small table with three plush chairs in the corner of the lobby. "Why don't we sit over there."

"Somewhere more private," Keith said, bypassing Terrance and instead looking directly at Marta. That icy stare had not changed. It was the look you gave a stubborn dog after demanding he sit. An *or else* quality to it.

"Right there is fine," Marta said, not waiting to see if anyone would follow as she moved toward the chairs. She picked the one that seemed easiest to jump from and leave in hurry.

Terrance was right by her side but she didn't look back to check on Keith. Unfortunately, he did follow and stood leaning against the back of the chair next to her.

"I don't see what this has to do with him," Keith replied,

gesturing with his head toward Terrance. "You and I can deal with our own problems."

"*We* don't have problems," Marta corrected quickly. "There is no *we*. You came here with something to say—let's hear it. Terrance is part of my team now that I'm advancing my career. You can say what you have to say, but it'll involve him."

Keith shook his head. "When did you start talking like that?" He chuckled sarcastically. "You sound like a little kid trying to play grown-up."

"Go to hell," Marta snapped wildly, surprising even herself. "You don't get to show up here unannounced and start making demands and crappy comments. Sit down and talk or leave. I don't actually care what you do, but get on with it."

Taken aback for a moment, Keith seemed to hold his breath. A moment later, he rounded the chair and sat down. Once Terrance saw him move, he did too, taking the third seat around the small table.

"You know what I have to say," Keith said in a hushed voice. "Your mother made it sound like you're about to break out and be some hot shit."

"She is," Terrance cut in. "And it doesn't need to have anything to do with you."

Keith twisted his face up. "I guess that depends on her. Our marriage isn't anyone's business. We have very different perspectives, and I don't want her putting a spin on it."

"I'm going to stop you there," Terrance asserted. His tone was unmistakable, and while Marta was grateful, she knew exactly how Keith reacted to a hostile approach. She wanted to explain exactly what needed to happen. You didn't walk haplessly through a minefield. You tiptoed quietly, holding your breath. Terrance was not as well-practiced at it as Marta, though he didn't seem rattled at all. "Keith, we're not here to rewrite history. All three of us have a problem to deal with. There is a documented history within the judicial system that anyone with basic investigative skills could expose. There is a tactful way to handle this. But it requires restraint, something I'm not convinced you have."

Keith's teeth ground together. "I'm not here for a lecture. Marta can try to play victim, but she's not dragging my name through the mud to do it."

"That's not what I'm doing," Marta insisted, but her voice faltered. "Keith, I don't want trouble. I've kept quiet all these years. I left and have not made a fuss about anything."

Terrance squirmed a bit in his chair. He didn't look thrilled at Marta's attempt at making amends. She didn't blame him; it bordered on groveling.

"Please don't act like you've been keeping some deep, dark secret on my behalf." Keith rolled his eyes and shook his head. "I don't know what she's been telling you."

"Everything," Terrance said flatly. "And frankly, that's what people will want to know. All the details. Every reporter who gets a tip about police reports and restraining orders will be looking for the tantalizing details. When a story like this breaks, it tends to snowball."

"Are you threatening me?" Keith boomed loudly enough to send his words echoing around the hotel lobby. All eyes turned their way.

"Marta is going to have a whole team of PR people and support from the foundation. Public opinion will most certainly favor her. Hell, if we polled everyone in this lobby and asked if they thought you were the problem around this table, I'm sure they'd agree you are. I don't think you've got the ability to keep it together. When the pressure's turned up, you blow. And that'll be all it takes to sink whatever life you've got here. What do you think people will say when they find out the kind of man you really are?"

Keith shot his finger out dangerously close to Terrance's face. "Don't mess with me," he sneered. "You have no idea what I can do."

"That's kind of the point, Keith, I do know. The problem for you is that your usual tactics don't mean a thing here. I have every resource at my disposal. You have threats and a temper. All things that will make you look worse. You can't even get through this conversation without puffing up your chest and acting ready for a street fight."

"I am ready." Keith's voice was still loud, and his nostrils flared with anger.

"I know you feel good when people are scared of you. That gives you some kind of rush. But you won't get that here. Not anymore. The best you can do is make a smart play. Find a way to make this work."

Keith's red face and clenched jaw brought Marta back to every misstep and ensuing argument of their marriage. All the burned dinners that resulted in broken dishes. The late returns from the grocery store that turned into interrogations. Terrance didn't seem to have the right amount of fear. He was poking the bear instead of playing dead.

"I'm not doing this," Keith announced loudly. "You don't get to come back to town after leaving me high and dry and start making demands. We still had that credit card with a few thousand on it, and I had to pay that off myself. You were just gone. Did we fight? Yes. But all couples fight. You can be dramatic about things. You have to admit that." He bore into Marta with a demanding stare. "You never just walked away when I wanted you to. It was always you needling me. Pushing me."

Terrance chuckled. "You might as well be writing the handbook for crap husbands who abuse their wives. You sound like an idiot, and no one is going to listen to what you have to say anyway. Let's settle this now. Marta is going to sign a contract that will launch her career. You are going to mind your business, keep your mouth shut, and let things happen for her. I will do my part to make sure nothing about your abuse comes to light. There are only a few people who know and minimal documentation. With the right pressure put in the correct places, I think we could seal those reports and ensure that the few people who do know are motivated to keep the information to themselves."

"You're so slick," Keith said, leaning back in his chair

and twisting his mouth into a forced smile. "You've got this all figured out."

"We can certainly do it your way." Terrance tossed up his hands and shrugged. "You want to just go duke it out in the hotel parking lot? One more obvious indication that you have zero self-control and are prone to violence. To be honest, the longer I sit here, the more I hope you do pick that option. I get to knock your ass out and you make my case for me."

"Knock my ass out." Keith laughed and then glared at Terrance.

Marta leaned forward and raised her hand to quiet them. "Stop this. Our marriage is over and it shouldn't impact the rest of our lives. It was a mistake. We never should have been together. We didn't stand a chance."

Keith looked as though a bright idea just struck him. "You wouldn't even have this opportunity if it weren't for me. I'm the only reason you have a life. Think of how much I helped you. Where would you be if I didn't do everything for you? You couldn't write a check, didn't know how to buy a car, or take care of a house."

"You did teach me that stuff," Marta admitted reluctantly. "Usually by yelling at me when I tried and did it wrong. But if I didn't know all those things, maybe I shouldn't have been married. I was in no place to play house and neither were you."

"And we were both to blame," Keith said, sounding like a car salesman trying to get her to sign on the dotted line. To agree to something he could hold her to later. "The fights we had were not what you always made them into, right?"

Terrance seemed ready to speak but instead he looked to her. There were so many moments she wanted to remind Keith of. Things he couldn't deny were way over the line. "If someone wants to come talk to you about me and our marriage, you just decline to speak. Whatever happens with my career, you don't have any say or any claim to anything."

"I think you meant to say thank you," Keith snarled sarcastically. "I took you on your first real vacation. I always made sure you had what you needed. You couldn't have run away and had a life if I hadn't done all that."

Terrance seemed unable to bite his tongue any longer. "You want a gold star? Because from my vantage point you can't be both hero and villain. Great, you took Marta on vacation for a week. How did that go? Did you treat her well? Any big fights or nasty comments? You don't get to set a house on fire and then get a round of applause because you threw a bucket of water on it."

"You told him about that," Keith looked wounded by this. "Marta, that was a bad night. We were partying. It's not what it sounds like."

She snickered and then huffed. "I didn't tell him that, Keith. He was being dramatic for effect. How could he possibly expect that you had actually poured gasoline all over our living room and threatened to burn it all down? You tried to board the door and swore you'd kill me in there. Kill us both. I got lucky that night and you punched some metal thing in the garage and broke your hand instead."

"You did something—" Keith began but then hesitated as he seemed to search his mind. "You were— I don't remember."

"Let me remind you," Marta said, the shake finally gone from her voice. "My friend Arlene and her boyfriend Brad were over. We had a fire out back and some drinks. You went in to go to the bathroom and Arlene went to get something from her car. A pack of cigarettes, I think. When you came back, Brad and I were alone in the backyard. In the same seats you left us in. Pretty far away from each other, actually. I remember that because I was trying to make sure you didn't get jealous. But unfortunately, we were talking to each other. That was enough for you to lose it."

"You'd been talking to him all night," Keith said, accusingly. "There was definitely something there."

"I was hosting my friend and her boyfriend and being kind to both of them. You threw them out, kicked the back door so hard it shattered the glass panel, went in the garage to get a board, a drill and a gas can, and you proceeded to terrorize me until you broke your hand and passed out. I didn't do anything to deserve that. Your own paranoia caused that, and your anger kept it going way over the line. The fact that you never killed me, still to this day, is surprising."

"You are so dramatic." Keith slapped his hand to his knee and his face burned red again. "That board wouldn't even hold the door, and there were about another ten ways out of the house. I didn't even have matches or anything on me. My lighter was still out in the backyard."

Terrance, who'd been listening with an expression of horror on his face, stood up abruptly. "Marta, we need to go. This is insanity, and you don't need to spend another second listening to him justify his obvious psychosis and abuse. You didn't cause that night and you didn't deserve it. Just because there was some other window you could jump out doesn't make it magically better. The fact that you think it does, Keith, makes me realize you're the exact same man you were then. I'm not worried at all if you want to go shout from the rooftops what you think about Marta or your version of events. Listening to you now, I know everyone will see you for exactly what you are. Good luck with that."

Marta stood, still feeling like things were unfinished here, maybe worse off than they were before. You didn't walk away from Keith when he was this angry. Turning your back made you vulnerable and he found it infuriating.

"You didn't even say what my options are," Keith called out anxiously. "Is there like a deal you're trying to make? Marta's mom said you gave her money."

Terrance stopped short and slowly turned, his face looking annoyed. "Why, Keith? Am I supposed to believe you're going to be able to hold up your end of anything? You're like a lit fuse, and I'm not spending all my time trying to extinguish it. I think I'd prefer to let you implode on your own."

Keith's posture changed. It would likely be imperceptible to most people, but everything was perceptible to

Marta. She was in tune with every raise of a brow or stiffening of the spine. This was Keith backing down. Something she'd never seen before. He had runaway train emotions. The kind that could only be stopped with some sort of force or destruction.

"I have a business here," Keith replied coolly. "I can't afford for my name to be dragged through the mud. I'm not that guy anymore, Marta. You did something to me. It was too intense. Maybe you're right that it wasn't the time for us. But I wanted it to be."

"Again," Terrance bit out angrily. He had not fully turned back to give Keith his attention. "Abuse is never deserved. Not by anyone. Not under any circumstance. We're not going to find common ground there. If you turned your life around, great. My only concern is Marta. Her safety and her future."

"Careful," Keith whispered then allowed his voice to grow larger. "She can bring out the worst in you."

Marta still wondered if that was true. Would Keith have been a better husband to a better wife?

Terrance ignored his comment. "Here's how this is going to work. A lawyer is going to draft a document for you to sign. It's going to ensure that you don't try to stake a claim to any of Marta's future success. She will agree to keep the details of your marriage to herself. The abuse will not be discussed publicly, and if the story does break for any reason, she'll minimize it. We'll come up with some canned responses that will block the press from probing further. It'll be a nonstarter."

Keith seemed to contemplate the idea as he cracked his knuckles in that old familiar way. "I don't see how I make out in this agreement. She's about to come into a whole bunch of money and I'm just supposed to keep my mouth shut for free?"

Marta, emboldened by the power shift, spoke up. "You lost any right to any part of my future the second you put your hands on me." She shook her head. "No, well before that. You were breaking me down long before you ever raised a hand to me. And I carry it all. Every single thing you said, all the times you iced me out or screamed in my face. Sometimes it's the first words I hear in the morning. It's the last thing I feel when I go to bed. I'm not done with you, and I'm scared out of my mind that I never will be. I long for the day that I walk around not flinching at the thought of you, not worried that somehow, some way you'll pop back up in my life. So you don't get to have any part of what I'm building. I'm making it on the ashes of what you burned down, and you're not getting a chance to do it again."

Stunned but quickly switching to ferocity, Keith stood up. His finger was pointed in her face and his eyes seeming to spin with anger. "And you think you're a big deal now. Like you can talk to me like—"

Terrance banged a hand to Keith's chest and Marta froze in fear. This would not go unanswered. There was no way to make the water stop boiling, the temperature cool. "No." That was it. That was all Terrance said. Like he was scolding a dog. She couldn't see Terrance's face, but Keith's changed dramatically as he took a step back.

"Never again," Terrance warned, his voice unforgiving and unwavering. "Not ever again."

Marta couldn't move. She might as well have been watching her parents fight or bracing for Keith's wrath on her. It was amazing how easy it was to forget to breathe. Terrance wrapped around her, ushering her toward the door. "I'm serious, Marta. It'll never happen again. I promise."

She nodded but couldn't accept his words as the truth. It always happened again. Either with her family or someone like Keith. There was always another explosion. Outburst. Flare-up of emotions. Table being flipped. Wall being punched. It never stopped. She'd tried to renew her life. Reset it. Run away. But here she was again. Sucked back in. The only thing tethering her to hope beyond this was Terrance's arm on her shoulder guiding her to the car. And she couldn't believe that would be enough to change things this time.

"I'll sign the contract," she uttered in some far-off voice as he pulled the car away from the curb and she looked in the rearview mirror. Keith stood on the sidewalk, his silhouette the same as she always remembered. "I need to move forward on this. I can't keep looking back."

Terrance laced his fingers in hers and squeezed gently. "Never again."

Marta kept her eyes fixed on the rearview mirror just long enough to see a woman close in on Keith and wrap her arms around him. She knew, from talking to her brother, there was someone else in Keith's life but seeing them together was somehow far more unnerving. Was she enough to make him whole? Or was she only his next punching bag? The answer shouldn't concern her. That was not her problem. Not her concern. But suddenly it seemed to matter deeply. She needed to know. She'd have to find out.

20

Carol

The staff was so discrete. They didn't make a peep. Robert and Carol had sat together, holding on for dear life, in front of a fire with a bottle of champagne. She'd spent her night talking out and reckoning with her father's choices. Robert had listened and chimed in about his own parents. Their hands were intertwined and their stories overlapped. Struggling against and moving toward the same rapture of trying to be both successful and worthy of success.

Their experiences were different, but at the core of it all was the desire to do better than what had come before. To leave a lasting impression on people who they cared about and try to improve what they could. When they'd come to that realization, a sense of peace fell over Carol.

Robert stretched as the last embers of the fire burned out. “I can’t think of the last time I stayed up all night and talked. Not since high school.”

“All-nighters are not part of my normal routine anymore either.” Carol laughed, watching Robert stand to his full height and stretch again. “The sun is coming up.”

“We haven’t even checked our phones,” Robert said, reaching for his and walking to the large bay window to watch the sun rise. “Looks like the world survived without me for a night.”

Carol grabbed her own phone and smiled. “Terrance texted this morning. It’s been tense out there, but Marta signed the contract. We have some work to do, but she’s on board.”

“You’re working incredibly hard to change things,” Robert said, smiling over his shoulder at her. “You should be proud.”

“Eli can do what he wants,” Carol asserted, sliding under Robert’s arm and resting herself against him. “I’m not my father; I can’t answer for him or his choices. All of that happened before I was born. Eli can come at me, and he’ll lose.”

“I’ve been making some decisions myself,” Robert announced happily. “I’m going to leave the board.”

“What?” Carol felt her heart skip a beat. Robert was a long-standing member of the board, and she wasn’t ready to lose him. Not in any capacity.

“I’ve always had a few other opportunities at other companies and have turned them down in order to remain with the Milton Cesar Foundation. It was an easy choice for me. I could do the work in my sleep, and the arts are a passion of mine. But it's time for me to move on."

"You can't," Carol pleaded. "I need your support in the coming months. Even if Eli doesn't win this battle, he'll still have his eye on the war. You're one of my strongest allies. I can't get this done without you."

"You won't be without me," Robert whispered. "But we both want to do the right thing, and we know that having a relationship and holding the positions we do is a conflict of interest. There is no gray area for that. We'd be putting everything you're trying to do at risk. It would destroy me to know that I left you vulnerable to losing what you've worked for."

"Then we'll just wait," Carol stuttered, taking a step back from him. The space between them felt suddenly cavernous and she wished to run to his arms once more. But that was the point. They couldn't. Not if they intended to continue working together. Robert was right, they would need to choose.

"I can't wait," Robert admitted with a smile. "I know I can't. You're the first thing that's come into my life in a long time that makes me feel that magic again. The divorce was hard. The kids going off to school was a challenge. But you—"

"I know," Carol's voice caught for a moment. "I feel that way too. But we've just started spending time together. It would be rash to alter your life so dramatically now."

"Normally, I'd agree." Robert moved closer and

caressed her cheek gently. "I'm very measured in my decision-making. But I also spent the entire night talking to you. And it doesn't seem like enough. I'm already dreading that I need to leave. Thoughts of you fill my day. I've been around long enough to understand something like this doesn't come around very often, and I'm not going to let one aspect of my career deter me."

"But I need your support on the board," she reiterated as she reached up and touched his hand on her cheek.

"I can be more to you than a vote across a conference room table. Let me be the person you come home and celebrate with when things go right. Let me be the person you lean on when it all goes wrong. The board position will be filled. You'll be as effective and persuasive as always. The only difference is we don't have to stop this." He gestured between the two of them. The potential of what they could be. Taking her hand up to his lips, he kissed it and smiled. "We have something here."

"I know," she sighed, a mix of defeat and relief. "I'm just terrified. The more I give space to my mother's memory and look back on how things really were, the more I have to face my own decisions. This fundamental barrier I've put between my love life and my career. I've always turned it into a choice. One over the other."

"You deserve both." He leaned down and kissed her lips briefly. "Maybe it's time. You don't have to choose anymore. You get to have both. I know it's a risk but I hope you're willing to take it with me."

Carol looked deep into his eyes and searched for an

ounce of doubt. The best she could tell, there wasn't any. And if she explored her own heart, the only apprehension she felt was about her career. Diving headlong into Robert's arms didn't worry her at all. Their conversations had depth; their attraction was palpable.

"So how would this work?" Carol asked, her words delicate, still desperately unsure. "What would we do exactly?"

"I would address the board. We'd be transparent and let them know that recently we've developed feelings for each other. In order to preserve the integrity of the board, I intend to step down, effective immediately. We're two single adults who are doing the right thing. People will understand, and I dare say maybe even be happy for us."

"Your optimism is adorable."

"And hopefully it's contagious." He held her again in his arms and stared down at her affectionately. "I think this will be worth it. You have the contract signed from Marta. You're on the right track. Now is the perfect time."

"Or is it you just can't wait any longer?"

He chuckled. "That too."

"I'll miss seeing you in the board meetings."

"But we can make all our own meetings. Special rendezvous. Much more fun than any board meeting."

"I can't believe we're going to do this." She shook her head and smiled wide. "I'll call a meeting for tomorrow. From the perspective of optics, the less time we let pass before letting people know, the better."

"I agree. My daughter Tasha will be thrilled. She adored

you and has been texting me regularly to see if I've gotten the courage to ask you out properly yet."

"We're acting like outrageous young people throwing caution to the wind." Carol gasped as Robert twirled her playfully and dipped her like a skillful dance partner.

"I'm ready to feel young again."

21

Marta

The second her pen had lifted off the contract, she felt the weight of the world press even harder on her shoulders. The choice itself was simple, but the implications would not be. Terrance had been strategic. He knew what he was doing. But she wasn't sure he'd weighed the cost.

They'd driven aimlessly for a little while and stopped at a coffee shop for her to sign the contract and him to electronically send it to Carol. When they'd gotten back to the hotel, Keith and the woman he was with were gone. They never made it past the lobby, lingering in the same spot they'd confronted Keith in.

"We should celebrate," Terrance suggested, trying to look upbeat. "Maybe dinner?"

"I don't think so," Marta apologized. "My head is swimming. It probably seems like you handled everything today. You were certainly more prepared than I realized. But the people we're dealing with never fail to be shockingly disappointing. I'm wrestling with a few things here."

"You regret signing the contract?" Terrance asked, looking worried. "I hope I didn't pressure you. It is time-sensitive, but it needs to be something you're certain about."

"You had a plan?" Marta asked, anxiety creeping up her spine and tingling her scalp. "Those documents for my mother to sign. You never told me about those."

"I didn't know if we'd use them." Terrance moved in closer but she felt herself lean away. "I had to meet your mom and try to decide what might sway her."

"And Keith? You went so hard at him. I told you that doesn't work for him. It was like you were baiting him."

"I was," Terrance explained calmly, not seeming to be pulled in to her swelling emotions. "I needed to see just how volatile he is. If he had any self-control or if he was easy to work up. It makes a difference in how we approach this. We have to be strategic. There are a lot of moving parts and varying personalities. If we want this to work, it's going to take a calculated approach. I'm sorry if it was upsetting to you."

"It's my life. It's my actual lived experiences. These are not chess pieces in a game. These are the people I've spend my adult life trying to cope with and avoid. Do you know what it did to me to sit across from him, watching you needle and waiting for him to explode. This might seem like it's all behind me, but it's not."

"I didn't consider that," Terrance admitted, looking instantly regretful. "I had my eye on the objective, and I didn't think about what it might do to you. But you have to know I wouldn't ever let anything happen to you. He will never touch you again."

"It's bigger than that." She wrapped her arms around herself and shrank down, slumping her shoulders. "There is more I have to protect myself from than him attacking me."

"Right," Terrance said, biting at his lip and seeming to think it all over. His dark eyes blinked slowly "I was being too tactical. Not realizing the impact of going hard at your mother and Keith. I just wanted to test the waters and see how they'd react. I'm sorry I put you in that position. I still think signing the contract was the right idea. And we certainly seemed to get Keith to some sort of an agreement."

"At what cost?" Marta asked, her throat closing at the prospects. "Aren't we signing a deal with the devil? Did you see her?"

"Who?" Terrance asked, trepidation filling his face.

"When we left and Keith walked outside, his girlfriend was there. She'd been obediently waiting for him to finish talking to me. If I go into some deal with him, swearing to keep it all a secret, what does that mean for her?"

"We don't know anything about their relationship. Plus I'm sure she's a grown woman. It's not your responsibility to deal with Keith anymore."

"If I know and do nothing," Marta whispered, covering

her face with her hands. "You're asking me to go into a legally binding contract with him that says I'll never tell anyone he's abusive."

Terrance nodded. "Yes, but in exchange for, essentially, your freedom from him. He can't come back and make a play for any money you make or slander you in anyway. You don't mess with him and he can't mess with you."

"His lies are not equal to my truth." Marta finally felt a surge of clarity. "Asking him to not come ruin my life with false attacks is not the same as asking me to be quiet about his violence and abuse. Those are not the same things."

Terrance nodded again; his eyes fixed on the ground. "I was trying to use leverage that he'd find compelling."

"And you did. What every abusive person wants is the ability to not be caught."

"I thought you wanted to bury this. When we talked it seemed as though it was something you didn't want to dig back up."

"Right now I don't. Or I didn't. Seeing that woman with him today as we drove away, it gave me pause. Have I done enough? Is staying quiet protecting me but putting other people at risk?"

"Those are important questions," Terrance agreed. "I don't know the answers."

"Me either," she said soberly. "But before we do anything formal with Keith, I need more time to figure it out."

"That's fair," Terrance agreed, perking up as if they'd

struck some kind of common ground that might make her feel better.

It didn't.

"I need a little bit," Marta said, tears forming in her eyes. "I'm going out for a while. You sent the contract to Carol. We're on the right track. I just need to clear my head."

"I can take you wherever you want to go," he shot back urgently. "I'm so sorry if I caused you any pain. I only want to help."

"I know you do," she said, furrowing her brows. "I knew once I started this, I'd have to face a lot of things I was running from. It's why I hesitated." She touched his arm gently and then moved away. "I'll be back later."

Terrance looked ready to protest but swallowed the words. With a small nod and wordless wave, she reached the curb outside. There was nowhere in particular she planned to go. It was more a feeling she was chasing. That icy relief of aloe on a sunburn. She was ablaze and something had to cool her down.

When she was a block away, she pulled out her phone. Without any hesitation she dialed.

"Eddy?" She choked out the words. "Can you come pick me up?"

He didn't ask. Eddy didn't pry and probe and try to sort it all out. He pulled up to the curb, leaned over to unlock his old truck door and let her climb in. The quiet was perfectly acceptable. Comfortable even.

"Remember this song?" he asked, turning the radio up a bit. "We played this to death. I tried to learn it on the guitar."

"You sucked at the guitar."

"I did."

The silence broken, she felt the words bubble up in her. "I'm sorry. I hope you weren't in the middle of something when I called. It was a really hard day and I just . . . Actually I don't know why I called you."

"Sometimes it's nice to have a familiar face when things go down." Eddy kept his eyes on the road and tapped fingers on the steering wheel to the song they used to love.

"Keith came around today," Marta explained. "It was really hard. I don't know why I kept this to myself so long. He was incredibly abusive and violent while we were married. I've hinted at it or alluded to it but saying it straight out is hard. I don't know why. Maybe I'm worried about how it reflects on me, or what might happen if he knows I'm talking about it."

"I'm sorry, Marta," Eddy offered. "I didn't know how bad it was. I'm glad you got away from him."

"I got away and then did nothing. All the little legal stuff I did, I never took it all the way. I was afraid it would make things worse. I ran away and now he's someone else's problem. Or maybe a problem for a lot of different people."

"He'll become your problem again too if you don't tread lightly. Keith and I don't hang around the same places but people know he's got issues. Not like you're talking about, but I don't think it would shock anyone to hear the truth."

"But I'm the one in the position to tell the truth. And I know it puts me in a greater risk."

"That's tough," Eddy sighed. "I wish things could be easy for you. Like, just for once, I wish it would work out with no problems."

"I guess that's too much to ask." Marta leaned her head against the window and watched the unforgiving world go by.

"You're screwed no matter what you do."

"Right."

"Running away worked for a while." He raised a brow as he seemed to give it all some thought. "Do you really need to be the winner of some award and a best-selling author?"

"I don't," Marta admitted. "Maybe it would make my life easier in the long run."

"The short term will suck." He smiled apologetically. "I'm not really a solutions kind of guy. But I can take you to the football field with a six pack and we can curse at the stars like we used to."

Her thoughts sprang back and forth between Terrance sitting alone at the hotel and Eddy offering some sentimental therapy. "I don't know what I want," she admitted quietly. "I hate not knowing what to do."

"Don't look at me." He tossed his hands up and laughed. "I procrastinate and ignore, hoping the hard decisions go away. Apparently, that's not a real good strategy. Like I said, the best I can do is distract you."

"That doesn't sound too bad right now." Marta checked her phone and closed her eyes. She hadn't been back to the high school football field in ages. A beer sounded perfect. "Maybe just a little while."

"You'll be all right Marta. You were always the best of all of us. At some point the world is going to have to give you a break."

"It's trying to," Marta said, "but I can't seem to figure out how to make it work."

22

Carol

At least there were two valid reasons to call the impromptu board meeting. Terrance had done it. He'd come through and found a way to convince Marta to sign the contract. They were locked in together now. The press release could be written. Production on the feature video segment for the award ceremony could begin. And she had good news for the board.

"Thank you all for coming. I'm sorry for the late notice. Those of you who are only able to call in, I hope our connection is clear."

Robert looked so confident and comfortable. Maybe because he didn't have to make the awkward announcement about his personal life. She would handle that. And the best part was Eli wasn't there. No one had been brave or stupid enough to try to invite him back after Carol had kicked him out last time.

Carol decided to lead with the news about Marta. "As you can see from the folders in front of you, Marta has signed the contract. We are now officially able to move forward with the process. As you know from the last meeting, this was the last roadblock in the planning phase for the next award ceremony. Everything else is well underway."

Larry, normally always looking displeased seemed to perk up a bit. "Should we expect things to be in line with our usual programing during the ceremony?"

Carol looked across the table at each of the board members, but landed on Robert last. "No. You should expect more people to tune in. More people feel seen and represented. Once it's publicly announced that Marta is the winner, I intend to ensure people know what makes her unique and how things will change going forward."

Larry rolled his eyes. "Can we stop acting like poverty is a whole personality. Or a skill. I get that you selected her so that she can be some tokenized beacon of hope. But really you're creating a false expectation for people who will never have a shot."

"Marta is not a token selection. She's a brilliant writer who has earned her spot here. She wouldn't be an anomaly at all if people with your thinking would pull some of the barriers down. I can't change history, but I can try to make improvements wherever possible. We all can. We all should."

"I agree," Robert said firmly. "If we're being honest with ourselves, we should have a great deal of self-reflection and in turn, remorse over how exclusive this foundation has been for years. The world looks to us for what is considered top in the market and we've been showing them this sliver of what's available."

Most heads in the room shook in agreement and the chatter from those calling in was positive.

"We have many more meetings on the calendar to discuss this," Carol reminded them. "There is one more thing I'd like to address. In the interest of full disclosure I would like to let everyone know that effective at the end of this week Robert will be stepping down from his position on the board."

"Why?" Larry asked, narrowing his eyes.

"Robert and I have recently been working on a project together and during that process have decided we'd like to pursue a relationship in our personal lives. This is not some long standing situation that we've kept secret. It is in fact very new. But we're acting quickly because we do not want there to be any perceived conflicts of interests. We're disclosing this now and making the changes needed to protect the foundation."

There were some smiles and nods. A few congratulatory well-wishers. And she was sure she heard a bit of grumbling too. "The normal process for replacing a board member will take place. I appreciate the timing is not ideal as we are in the midst of so many changes but I have confidence in what we're building."

Larry grimaced. “You’re leaving so you can date her? I don’t understand.”

“I wouldn’t expect you would,” Robert shot back.

Carol held up a hand. “There is one more thing.” The group muttered some jokes and she waved them off. “I know. It’s a lot all at once but that’s how it works around here. I wanted to disclose something I recently learned.” She looked at Robert for reassurance. They hadn’t discussed this. Up until a moment ago she hadn’t been sure she’d disclose it all. Something just felt right. Robert gave her a little nod before she began to speak. “While cleaning out my parents’ things, I discovered something about my father. Apparently, before I was born, my father was a member of the TRB. For those not familiar, it was a political group that was eventually disbanded. The practices and beliefs of this group do not align with any of my personal values. As I said, my father left this group prior to my birth and many of you know from his long career, he was infamous for being an inclusive, forward-thinking man. I don’t have more information about his time in the group or his overall involvement. I also haven’t decided if I plan to share the information more broadly, but I did want each of you to be aware. Personally, it’s been a lot to take in and honestly I’m still processing it but—”

The door to the board room swung open and Eli marched in, chest puffed out, shoulders arrogantly pushed back. “I’m interrupting, but for a good reason.”

“Excuse me?” Carol asked, hopping to her feet. “We’re

in the middle of a meeting. I made it perfectly clear last time—"

"You'll all want to hear this," Eli said, moving to the head of the table by Carol and smiling his pudgy-faced grin. "Before you continue to follow your flawless leader here, I think there are a few things you should know. She may be portraying herself as pristine and without any skeletons in her closet, but I promise you she has many." He pointed to Robert who looked ready to toss him out any second. "These two have been meeting in private under the guise of working on business. In fact it's far more than that. A relationship between a board member and the CEO of a foundation like this is completely unacceptable. Grounds to part ways with said CEO if you ask me. She's welcoming all sorts of drama and scandal onto us already with all the changes she's trying to make. Now she's disgracing her position by carrying on with Robert."

The room was silent for a moment. People looked to each other and then some chatter broke out on the phone in the center of the table. Finally Lori spoke up. "Eli, Carol and Robert have already disclosed this to us and he plans to step down which seems like a perfectly reasonable solution. What is highly inappropriate is you, someone not on this board, storming in with the intention of discrediting our current CEO."

Stunned, Eli searched the room for an ally. Charles, who normally did his bidding, was quiet and looking away.

Carol gestured for the door. "Please let's not make me

asking you to leave become a habit, Eli. We're in the middle of a meeting."

"You are about to be embroiled in more of a mess than you can imagine," Eli pressed, now sounding frantic. "Do you know what kind of family she comes from? Do you know what she grew up with?"

Robert stood and shook his head. "Eli, you've got nothing here. You need to leave before we call security. I know you've been working overtime to try to undermine Carol and the work she's doing. The only tactic you have is to twist stories and use blackmail. Your time is over."

Eli chuckled, planting his feet. "The TRB. Her father was practically a founding member of the TRB. How do you think that's going to look when a few national papers get a hold of the story? This woman, pioneering all this change and crap is really no more than a closeted extremist pushing for the values of TRB."

There were laughs and Lori spoke again. "Eli, she disclosed this to us as well. And what you're talking about happened before she was born. She can't answer for her father's choices and no newspaper out there is going to ask her to. The only thing we can measure Carol on is her own personal work to counter groups like the TRB and men like you who try to make sure foundations like this don't allow anyone else in."

Eli shook his head. "A newspaper will pick up any story with enough meat to it. I can certainly find people willing to go on record and disparage your father and his associates. If you think they can't find links to you and whatever social circles you were in growing up, you're naïve. I am sure you attended some ball or won some cotillion prize that links back to the TRB. Maybe there are even some pictures someone snapped. That wouldn't play well."

"You're grasping for straws," Robert snarled angrily. "Is this really what you want to do? Some weak swipe at someone who is dominating you in every other arena. It's pathetic. The wheels of change are in motion, get out of the way or get run over."

Larry cleared his throat. "I think you need to cool it, Eli. I see what you're trying to do, but I don't know that it's going to reflect well. That's what we're tasked to do. Ensure the success of not one person, but the foundation as a whole. I'm not saying I agree with every idea Carol is proposing but I am willing to watch it unfold. At the end of the day her success is our success. Actively trying to undermine her only causes more problems for everyone."

Carol was stunned by the show of support. "Eli, you tell whatever story to whatever paper you want. Spin lies. Try to disparage my dead father. Maybe some people will buy what you're selling. I can't control that. All I can do is try to live up to the values my father actually instilled in me. The ones I believe he grew to hold at a high regard. You can do what you like, but do it elsewhere."

Eli's face turned a fiery red as he scanned the room again for an ally. He fixed on Charles, who continued to squirm. "You're all obsessed with this idea of change. The way things have always been is some disaster you're trying to save everyone from. I am so sick and tired—"

With a thud to the door, security walked in and surveyed the room. “Ma’am, should we start an escort out?”

“That’s up to him,” she said, gesturing toward Eli. “He’s welcome to leave on his own accord.”

“You just keep pushing,” Eli said, moving to the door on his own. “You really don’t know what you’re getting into.”

“Why? Do you plan to start mailing more dead rats to my office?” She rolled her eyes and tipped her chin to the security officer who looked most excited to see some action. When he made his move, Eli retreated the rest of the way.

The room looked ready to erupt in applause but instead they sat buzzing with some unused energy. Carol knew how to harness that. “There is always going to be someone trying to slow us down or distract us. We can’t let that happen. Let’s recommit ourselves to the agenda I know will be successful.” She locked eyes with Robert and knew this would likely be the last time she had him in her corner in this room. But there was no limit to what might come next for them in the outside world.

He winked and sent a shiver of excitement through her. Glancing down at a copy of the contract Marta had signed, she felt as if everything was falling into place and she’d finally have someone to celebrate with. Her mother’s voice tried to creep in. Reminders of the impossible and the customary. But she held them at bay. There were enough tangible things that could derail her plans, no need to conjure up old memories too. The focus had to be on the future. On Marta’s success. On Robert’s affection. On the chance to fulfill her destiny. In that there was great hope.

23

Marta

Everything was smaller. She'd remembered the bleachers by the football field as these huge looming steel mountains. The school building in the distance was not at all as enormous as she remembered either. Years had a way of shrinking down the places that were once so overwhelming and insurmountable.

"I haven't been back here since graduation." Marta took a long look around as Eddy spun the top off a beer and handed it over. "Nothing is how I remember it."

"Really?" Eddy asked, sounding shocked. "I'm out here all the time so it's exactly how I remember it."

"What do you come out here for?" Marta asked fixing her eyes on Eddy's kind face. His mannerisms were just how she remembered them. The hand she once held seemed just as calloused and hard working as the last time he'd laced his fingers with hers.

"We all hang out here sometimes. Just you know, the crew of townie folks with nothing better to do. Once the bar closes, we roll out here. The cops leave us alone as long as we don't get so loud that we wake up the Certas."

"The Certas still live back there?" Marta asked, wondering if she'd be part of that townie crew hanging out here if she hadn't left. Would Eddy be spinning the top off her beers and parking his truck close enough so he could play their favorite songs?

"Old man Certa is ninety-three. I swear he's never going to croak. That's why we don't get in trouble for hanging out here anymore because he's super deaf now. But I'm sure you're doing much better stuff where you live. You got friends up there?"

"Yeah," Marta said, smiling at the thought of her dear friends. Heather and Ray, who were dating each other now, had been endlessly loyal to her. She'd been lucky to find them. "I've got a couple of really good friends I met at work. We all watch out for each other."

"Good. You deserve nice people around you. I heard you're in town with some guy, Terrance or something?"

Her cheeks pinked. She had no reason to be embarrassed. She was not beholden to either of these men. Yet she suddenly felt uneasy, like she'd been keeping a secret. "He works for the foundation. Terrance has been trying to help me figure out how to navigate everything."

"And he's hot," Eddy laughed. "Or at least that's what the girls at the bar were saying. You know how the rumor mill works around here. Is he a good guy?"

"He seems like it," Marta shrugged, sipping on her beer to delay having to say anymore.

"You like him?" Eddy pressed, waggling his brows playfully. "I can tell you do so don't lie."

"Even if I did, we are in the middle of this big mess with the award. It wouldn't make sense to complicate it even more with a relationship."

"Screw that," Eddy teased. "Love waits for no one. If you like him you need to just go for it. And don't talk about this super spiffy award like it's a problem. Think of all the people who'd sell their left nut for the chance to do what you're doing."

Marta missed the brashness of this kind of conversation. No one painted a picture more vividly than a New Englander who'd had a few beers. Crude and silly, but familiar and funny.

"If you're so sure I should make a move with Terrance, why take me out to this very secluded and nostalgic spot? Aren't you making your move?" Her heart was curious and she was feeling bold.

"I had my day with you," Eddy said, now it was his turn to blush. "But you're destined for much bigger and better things than anything in this town. Including me."

"You're a great guy," she protested. "You were then and you are now."

"Fine," he shrugged. "But I made the mistake of

thinking I was what you needed back then. I make a lot of mistakes but I try not to make the same one twice. You've got a chance here at something amazing. The best thing I can do is make sure you take it."

"What if that's not what I want?" She dropped her head and stared at her shoes. "What if I want to go back to what my life has always been?"

"Then hopefully all the people who care about you will slap you silly until you wake up and realize how dumb that is. I don't care if you date this Terrance guy or not. That's up to you. But if you just go back up to that town you moved to and hide away, then you're really letting yourself down. Not to mention all the people you can help by becoming a success."

"You're so sure I will be successful?"

"Yes," he said, unequivocally. "You already are. You're just the last person to get the memo about it. Any time you want, I'll come pick you up and drive you out to the old places we used to go. We can listen to the songs we loved. I can even want to kiss you." He winced. "Desperately. But I'm not ever going to be the reason you shrink your world down. I'm not going to be the place you hide. Not when the thing you're hiding from is a shot at happiness."

"Damn," she grimaced. "When did you get so deep?"

"My grandma, you remember her?"

"Yeah," Marta chuckled, thinking of the old hunchback woman who would send them home with random things from her fridge every time they visited. "She was a hoot. When did she pass?"

"Four years ago. She lost her mind. Dementia. It was sad to watch. But in all the nonsense she talked, there were really important things I tried to hang on to. It kind of changed how I look at things."

"That's really sweet. I'm glad she had you with her in the end."

"It was hard," he admitted. "Watching the light dim out of someone slow like that, it's sad. But we'd sit on her front porch and she'd just talk. One day we were watching this bird's nest. It had been out in one of her plants for a while and finally the baby birds hatched. It gave us something to do a for a while. For a week straight I'd pretend I was coming to check on them instead of check on her. One by one the little feathery blobs worked up the energy to fly out of the nest. She was so happy." He took a long swig of the beer and she watched him relive the memory, pain and joy painting his face. "I was disappointed to see them go. I asked her, don't you wish they'd stay a little longer so we could keep watching them? Maybe one will fall and we can help it."

"You were always such a softy for animals," Marta recalled.

"My grandmother came over, put her hands on my cheeks. I won't ever forget how she explained it to me. She said, they aren't here for us. The best thing they can do is learn to fly. When they don't fly, they hit the ground. When the birds fall, they stay longer, but they're never the same. Maybe we'd have to pick it up, put it in a shoe box, feed it and nurse it back to health. We'd feel like we really accomplished something. We fixed it. But the best thing we can do is hope they all leave. Even if we're sad they're gone. Gone is better than broken."

"You remember that so vividly." Marta watched his face change from somber to joyful.

"It's a good lesson. I lost her two weeks later. And I just kept thinking about what she said. Sometimes it hurts to see people leave and let them go. I feel like she knew her time was coming and she wanted me to let her go. Now you're sitting here. On the edge of the nest. You've got your wings. Even if, selfishly, I wanted you to stay around longer it wouldn't be right. I've gotten better at letting things and people go when it's best for them."

Marta nodded, the words sinking deep into her heart. "I think a part of me is hoping I fall on my face and someone gets to scoop me up and keep me caged a while."

"I can tell." He finished his beer and waved for her to follow. "You don't need to be hanging around the old football field and thinking about this place anymore. You've got something better waiting for you. Maybe someone better. I don't know that guy. But I know what your face looked like when you talked about him. That's got to count for something."

"Terrance is a good man."

"You're due for one of those." He rolled his eyes. "Come on, let me give you a ride back to the hotel. If he's such a good guy, then he'll be worried."

"I still love you Eddy," Marta admitted confidently.

"Maybe it's a twisted sentimental love rooted in gratitude and not reality. But it's there."

He put his hand over his heart looking all at once flattered and wounded. "That means so much to me. And I get it. I feel it too. Whatever it is. Which is why I'm dropping you back off now before the beer convinces me I'm an idiot for letting you go."

Marta sighed and then smiled. He was right. In just about everything, he was right. It was time to go. Time to give in to the future she'd been trying to dodge and avoid.

24

Marta

Eddy's guess was spot on. Terrance did in fact look terrified when she arrived back at the hotel. Pacing the lobby, a wash of relief seemed to flow over him when she walked in.

"I'm sorry," she announced, falling into his arms. "I shouldn't have taken off like that. I was freaked out."

He held her tightly and didn't say a word for a long time. Finally, seeming to gather himself he spoke. "I'm glad you're ok. I was worried you went to confront Keith or just ran off. I don't want to lose you."

"I know this is a big deal for your career and for Carol."

"No," Terrance cut in, "I just don't want to lose you in my life. If you said right now you couldn't do it. That you wanted to run and never look back. The only thing I'd want is to come with you."

She chuckled nervously. "You don't mean that. This is your life. Your career. I'm the lynch pin that's holding it all up."

"You're more than that. I sat here thinking about what I asked you to do. I'm telling you that you have to bury your past in order to have a future. You have to pretend and keep quiet for a man like Keith to leave you alone. I hear myself saying it and I'm just—"

"I understand how we got there," Marta said quietly into his shoulder, still in his arms. She never wanted to let go. "You were trying to find the best way through it. The least messy. Logical."

"That doesn't mean it's the right way." He leaned back and looked down at her sincerely. "If you want to go at him head on, then we do that. If you want to take him on, we can."

"I don't know yet," she said, dropping her head down. "Before I thought I just wanted to put it all behind me. Now that I've seen him again, I can't imagine not speaking up."

"We don't have to decide now," Terrance said comfortingly. "I'm just glad you're back. You looked ready to run."

"I was," Marta said with a tiny smile. "But my friend Eddy reminded me I don't have run, I can fly."

"You can," Terrance agreed brightly. "And you will. I'll take your lead. Just tell me what you want to do next."

She raised to her tip toes and kissed him, her hand on his cheek holding him there. He didn't need the help. He wasn't going anywhere. Without hesitation he engaged fully in the kiss, and she moaned with passion and relief. Stepping back she planted a hand on his chest. "I know I want to be happy. And brave. And at peace. I think I'd like you to be around too."

"I'm going where you go. I'm fighting whatever battles you want. I promise."

Marta leaned her head against his chest and listened to his heart thud. For the first time she wasn't trying to find refuge in someone. Not searching for someone to slay her dragons, but someone to hand over her sword. Marta was ready to stop running and save herself. Turn and face the danger. The fear of failure. The hordes of people who might want to bring her down. She'd look them all dead in the eyes and fight.

"Excuse me ma'am?" The woman working the front counter came over with a large shipping envelope in her hands. "You're Marta Leduc right? This Package was delivered for you today."

Marta looked to Terrance before reluctantly taking the envelope. "From who?"

"It came by courier," the woman explained with a shrug. "I'm not sure. No return address." She hurried away to answer the ringing phone behind the front desk.

Terrance groaned. "Well that's not a good sign. Let me open it."

"If it's a bomb I don't think it'll matter which one of us opens it."

"It could be a rat."

"Feels too small for a rat." She ripped into the top of the envelope and held her breathe. Nothing happened. Peering inside she saw a small USB drive. Nothing else. "What do you think is on this?"

"Nothing good." Terrance took it in his hand and examined it closely. No markings. No indication of what might be on it. "Maybe we should just throw it in the trash."

"No," Marta said, straightening up. "We're ready for whatever it is. Right? Together."

"Right," Terrance said, looking wholly unconvinced. "I'm sure it's family photos or a nice poem congratulating you on your award."

"Hey, I'm the one who is supposed to be pessimistic."

"I know. But this, whatever it is, I'm sure is the last thing we need right now." He dropped his head into his hand and grumbled something else.

"Want to run away?" She smiled and touched his chest again. "We can go right now. Never look back."

He met her smile with his own and lifted his head back up. "Come on, let's go fire up a computer and see what we're working with."

"We can handle it." She felt good to be the one leading the charge. Propping him up. "Or we'll go hide out on a beach somewhere forever. Either way." She shrugged playfully and took his hand. This was all far more optimistic than she really felt. The looming question of who sent the drive and what might be on it was actually terrifying. But it was her turn to carry them through tonight. Tomorrow they could switch off. And Maybe that would be the best they could do. Seesaw their way through the worst of it. Rising and falling, taking turns at being strong. Maybe that was what a relationship was all about. She had a feeling her theory was about to be put to the test. She was never very good at taking tests.

The End

ALSO BY DANIELLE STEWART

Missing Pieces Series:

Book 1: The Bend in Redwood Road

Book 2: The Pier at Jasmine Lake

Book 3: The Bridge in Sunset Park

Book 4: The Stairs to Chapel Creek

Book 5: The Cabin on Autumn Peak

Brave Moments Series:

Book 1: Anywhere the Weeds Grow

Book 2: Anytime the Birds Fall

Book 3: Any Place the Sun Rises

Piper Anderson Series:

Book 1: Chasing Justice

Book 2: Cutting Ties

Book 3: Changing Fate

Book 4: Finding Freedom

Book 5: Settling Scores

Book 6: Battling Destiny

Book 7: Unearthing Truth

Book 8: Defending Innocence

Book 9: Saving Love(includes excerpts from Betty's Journal)

Edenville Series – A Piper Anderson Spin Off:

Book 1: Flowers in the Snow

Book 2: Kiss in the Wind

Book 3: Stars in a Bottle

Book 4: Fire in the Heart

Piper Anderson Legacy Mystery Series:

Book 1: Three Seconds To Rush

Book 2: Just for a Heartbeat

Book 3: Not Just an Echo

Broken Mirror Series:

Book 1: The Way Down

Book 2: The Way Home

Book 3: The Way Back

The Clover Series:

Hearts of Clover - Novella & Book 2: (Half My Heart & Change My Heart)

Book 3: All My Heart

Over the Edge Series:

Book 1: Facing Home

Book 2: Crashing Down

Midnight Magic Series:

Amelia

Rough Waters Series:

Book 1: The Goodbye Storm

Book 2: The Runaway Storm

Book 3: The Rising Storm

Stand Alones:

Yours for the Taking

Love in a Paper Garden

****

Multi-Author Series including books by Danielle Stewart

All are stand alone reads and can be enjoyed in any order.

Indigo Bay Series:

A multi-author sweet romance series

Sweet Dreams - Stacy Claflin

Sweet Matchmaker - Jean Oram

Sweet Sunrise - Kay Correll

Sweet Illusions - Jeanette Lewis

Sweet Regrets - Jennifer Peel

Sweet Rendezvous - Danielle Stewart

Short Holiday Stories in Indigo Bay:

A multi-author sweet romance series

Sweet Holiday Wishes - Melissa McClone

Sweet Holiday Surprise - Jean Oram

Sweet Holiday Memories - Kay Correll

Sweet Holiday Traditions - Danielle Stewart

BOOKS IN THE BARRINGTON BILLIONAIRE SYNCHRONIZED WORLD

By Danielle Stewart:

Fierce Love

Wild Eyes

Crazy Nights

Loyal Hearts

Untamed Devotion

Stormy Attraction

Foolish Temptations

Surprising Destiny

Lovely Dreams

Perfect Homecoming

You can now download all the Barrington Billionaire books by Danielle Stewart in a "Sweet" version. Enjoy the clean and wholesome version, same story without the spice. If you prefer the hotter version be sure to download the original.

The Sweet version still contains adult situations and relationships.

Fierce Love - Sweet Version

Wild Eyes - Sweet Version

Crazy Nights - Sweet Version

Loyal Hearts - Sweet Version

Untamed Devotion - Sweet Version

Stormy Attraction - Sweet Version

Foolish Temptations - Sweet Version - Coming Soon

FOREIGN EDITIONS

The following books are currently available in foreign translations

German Translation:

Fierce Love

Ungezügelte Leidenschaft

Wild Eyes

Glühend heiße Blicke

Crazy Nights

Nächte, wild und unvergessen

Loyal Hearts

Herzen, treu und ehrlich: Die Welt der Barrington-Milliardäre

***

French Translation:

Flowers in the Snow

Fleurs Des Neiges

NEWSLETTER SIGN-UP

If you'd like to stay up to date on the latest Danielle Stewart news visit www.authordaniellestewart.com and sign up for my newsletter.

AUTHOR CONTACT INFORMATION

Website: AuthorDanielleStewart.com
Email: AuthorDanielleStewart@Gmail.com
Facebook: facebook.com/AuthorDanielleStewart
Twitter: @DStewartAuthor
Bookbub: https://www.bookbub.com/authors/danielle-stewart
Amazon: https://www.amazon.com/Danielle-Stewart/e/B00CCOYB3O